3 1331 00784   W9-COH-668

MAY   2014

Platinum Dust

Part One

Written By: K.C Blaze

NO LONGER PROPERTY OF
Missouri River Regional Libr.

Missouri River Regional Library
214 Adams Street
Jefferson City, Missouri 65101

Platinum Dust

Copyright © 2011 by K.C Blaze

All rights reserved. No part of this book may be reproduced or transmitted in any form or by any means without written permission of the author.

ISBN 978-0615999081

Dedication.

I want to take a moment to thank a few special people who both inspired and motivated me to complete the mission. I would like to thank my family Elijah, Monay, Allana and Roberto for listening to me go over the story again and again. For also giving me advice and helping me craft the best characters and storyline ever. A special thanks goes to a friend Ashley Anderson who was the best guinea pig ever. You not only motivated me to finish but your insatiable desire to read the finish product inspired me to work harder than I planned. A big thank you also goes out to my mother for believing in my writing abilities and my sister's Paris and Tiffany for investing in my dream. Dad, you being proud of me means more than you will ever know.

Another special thanks goes out to all of the fans of the Urban Fiction genre. Keep reading and I will keep producing.

Table of Contents

Chapter One:
The Playa's Playground

Raheim Starz

It's one thing to talk a lot of smack but it's completely different to live it. See I'm that dude who keeps the ladies wet at night make em fall out calling on Jesus to bring em water because I'm so hot. My name is Raheim Starz and yes that's my real name. Tonight I'm lying in bed with my Tuesday night and although it's Friday she called me begging. Her name is Kelly and she's a red bone tall, thin, small tits but an ass like a donkey so that's why I came on through. Everybody has a preference, which usually includes the light skinned honeys at the top of the list, but my preference is the chocolate sistahs or the honey colored chicks with the thick hips. Kelly ain't a dime but my motto goes "Pussy don't have a face only a smell and a taste" so I don't discriminate.

I could hear the water running in the bathroom next to the bedroom door so I knew she was giving herself a quick wash down something she should have done before I got here. I don't claim to be God's great gift but I'm never pressed. My looks have carried me since I was in diapers.

1

My 6'4 frame is appreciated by both men and women alike, and my light brown complexion looks like I have a 365-day tan. My jet-black hair is thick and curly but I like to keep it in cornrows that I have done for free on an every three-day basis. I'm not one to hit the gym but for dramatic effect I do 300 sit-ups and 300 pushups a day to keep my body tight. My best feature is my green eyes. Yeah I'm pretty but don't let my looks fool you. I'm quick to grip a niggas ass up. Especially if he thinks I'm soft.

"Yo Kelly, I'm about to bounce" She was going to interfere with my original Friday and that ain't about to happen. See Friday belongs to Felicia her fine ass is as dark as night. Her hair is naturally long and black with auburn tint. Her smile is enough to get my wood excited. She has a body that God created only to show off with a small waist, thick legs and tits that set it all off. Felicia topped everybody. I could sit and pretend she was wifey not press her for sex and treat her like everybody treats me. Spoiled!!!! What I like most about her is that she is funny as hell and she doesn't sweat me like these other chicks do.

Kelly swung the bedroom door open wearing a pink tank top and white boy shorts, the ones I love, that show the bottom of her ass.

"You ain't going nowhere," she said, "I ain't tell you? I'm keeping you for the night" I decided not to correct her until after I got what I came here for. She straddled me and it was times like this that made me wish she had tits. Her hips started gyrating to a silent tune while she unbuckled my belt.

"You real happy to see me huh?" I leaned my back against the wall because she didn't have a headboard so I could get a better look.

"I missed you baby. I get crazy when I don't see my man" Her man? I couldn't help but laugh she was trying to claim a nigga after I already told her we're only friends with benefits and since I only see her once a week its more benefits than friendship.

"Your man? When did I become your man?" I asked with a smile still on my face.

"When you started coming over here to fuck me." She stopped moving and gave me a death stare. I didn't need this shit tonight especially when I came to play. I put my arms around her waist and started kissing her on her neck. Her body as stiff as a board waiting for me to confirm that I was hers. I did what I do best and dodged the bullet.

"Listen baby right now I want to enjoy you ok? We're gonna talk about that later" She didn't move for a minute until I started kissing her neck.

"Ok but don't fuck with me Raheim" or what? I thought. Tonight is the last night I'm coming over here. The mistake most men make is to lie and say they belong to somebody. I tell everybody I mess with that I don't have a girlfriend and don't want one. Relationships are too much drama and rules that I don't have the patience to follow. She started getting real hype bouncing up and down and I ain't have my pants off yet. I stood up knowing I looked good in my fresh white button down and dark blue Roca Wear jeans. She started taking my shirt off while I reached for the condoms in my pants pocket.

"You don't need a condom tonight. I'm on the pill" she talked through kisses on my stomach.

"That's cool babe, but I never go out in the rain without my umbrella" She stopped again this time eyes on fire

"What? You don't trust me?"

"Hell NO!" I was dead serious I've been down here before every girl and their mama tryna have my baby. I had one girl say she had condoms only to find out that she poked 16 holes in the tip. Calling me six o'clock in the morning crying, talking about "I'm pregnant" like she ain't plan the shit. I was at her door acting like a mad man. I gripped her ass up and dragged her to the nearest clinic. I don't believe in abortions or at least I didn't until I realized that I would have to deal with Tanisha's trifling ass for a life time and besides I couldn't love a kid knowing their mom set me up.

"Then why are you here if you don't trust me?"

"Because you called me."

I started buckling my belt I just didn't have the energy.

"Where you going?" she snapped

"I'm gone, it's obvious you on some other shit tonight, I didn't come here to be aggravated" I put my Timbs back on tucking my strings in. She started to panic

"You don't need to leave I'm sorry"

"It's cool, some other time" She ran over to her bedroom door trying to block it.

"Kelly move, I'll be back next week when you've taken your medicine"

"Don't do that"

"Do what?"

"Try to play me Raheim; I said I was sorry damn. You can wear the condom I don't care"

"See that's the thing baby girl you turned me off so watch yourself" I lifted her by the waist and moved her from in front of the door. She started following me out of the apartment complex talking loud.

"Please stay, I said I was sorry," I didn't answer nor did I stop which, made her act crazier.

"Don't come back then nigga, you leave now I don't want you coming back" She tried to raise her voice so I stopped for a moment catching the look of satisfaction on her face.

"Alright then" I kept going and she started crying.

"Why you acting all serious? You know I'm only playing" I walked to my black Expedition with the iced out rims and sped off. I saved myself a shower. I checked my cell phone to see how many calls I missed. Most of them from my Monday and Thursday girls. They both acted desperate too and that's why I'm about to cut them off. I pressed # 1 to speed dial Felicia, she answered on the third ring anybody else and I wouldn't have heard the phone ring.

"Hello?"

"Hey, do you mind if I come over now?" I tried not to sound hype.

"Well right now my girls are here. They want to go out tonight." I felt jealous but I wasn't saying nothing.

"Oh alright, maybe I'll check you later then"

"We'll be at club Six-Nine; if you want you can meet me there"

"Tell his fine ass to be there," one of her girlfriends shouted in the background.

"You already know I don't do the club thing, especially Six-Nine. You too good to be going to that cheap ass place." I didn't mean to sound frustrated but I wanted to see her.

"I know, and why you sounding all jealous? Last time I checked we didn't have any strings and anyway my girl Beverly is getting married"

"So yall go to a club?" I knew she'd appreciate my sarcasm. She said

"Exactly." Before starting to laugh.

"I have to go but I want to see you" This drove me crazy. I hated being surrounded by a bunch of suckas who started hating as soon as my foot hit the door. Some of them tried to test me by spilling drinks on my clothes so they could catch me out there. But I didn't have anything else to do and I really did want to see her.

"A'ight, about what time?" She told me to be there around eleven. I glanced at my platinum and diamond Cartier watch. I had to wait three hours. I made a quick decision to check out my aunt. She raised me and my baby brother. My mom's crazy ass is locked up for life she killed my dad when I was eleven after she found him laid up with an Italian broad. I was done with her ass the year before when she kicked me out for looking like my pops. You heard me right eleven years old with nothing but my busted bobos and superman t-shirt. I cried for a long time out on the concrete steps of our apartment building before I remembered my dad's sister. I walked half the day to get to Yeadon before I reached her suburban house going purely off of memory. When I told my aunt what happened she started crying and dialed my mom on the phone calling her every bitch in the book. She had custody over me and my brother a year later.

I didn't need to use my key because she never locked her door.

"Anybody home?" I stepped into the living room. The TV was on in the kitchen. I bought her a 52' flat screen for her birthday last year and she still chose to record and watch her trash shows on the outdated 13' in the kitchen.

"I'm in here." I gave her a kiss on her forehead before sitting at the table across from her.

"What you watching?"

"Maury, I swear I don't understand you young people. Why in the hell would anybody want to have nine men take a DNA test?"

"It's all about publicity, you don't know that?" I asked sarcastically.

"Your brother was here yesterday" Her eyes never left the screen.

"Janet sent him a letter last week. She wants him to come visit," She continued.

"His crazy ass can if he want to. Excuse my language but she'll see me on judgment day when God show her how she did me" My aunt knew how I felt about my mom and she never forced me to change my mind.

"I understand, Amir said he gonna check with you first" I stood up looking around the pots she had sitting on top of the stove changing the subject abruptly. "What's cooking?"

"I knew your greedy ass didn't come here to see me, get you a bowl out of the cabinet and get some of that spaghetti."

"How old is it?" I joked with her.

"About as old as your mouth" she swatted me on the back with her hand.

"Seriously though, she ain't been tryna to talk to us and all of a sudden 15 years later and you want a heart" I ate the spaghetti as fast as I put it in the bowl. The one thing I could say about my aunt is that Sadie can cook.

The phone rang on the kitchen wall. I grabbed it before she could.

"Hello? Who's calling?"

"It's Valerie, who's this Amir?"

"No it's Raheim and for that Ms. Val my moms can't talk to you" Ms. Val was my aunt's best friend and she helped my aunt and uncle look after us whenever she could when we were growing up.

"Boy if you don't give me my damn phone" She snatched the phone out my hand

"I know he done gone and went crazy" She laughed into the receiver while I took the chance to take a nap in my old room. I took the spiral staircase in the kitchen. Nothing changed. My real, dark wood bed frame still looked new except for the heart with my initials and my first love Cassandra Norman's carved into the bedpost. The posters of bikini-clad chic's posing on motorcycles were still plastered all over the walls. My dresser holding my trophies from track needed to be dusted. My Uncle Billy pulled me to the side one day and said getting the local honeys was cool but I needed to step up my game and join a sport. I told him track because I'd need to run from all of the ladies. At the time I didn't know how true that really was.

Janet Starz

Sitting in my cell waiting for the overweight C.O to do a head count I contemplated my next move. I need to win over Raheim or I would be here for another ten years.

"Janet Starz?" The C.O yelled out.

"I'm still here" I liked being sarcastic.

"A simple here is sufficient Mrs. Starz" She always said Mrs. When I irritated her trying to remind me of why I'm here. I don't need a reminder; every day in this hellhole reminds me that Carlos' ass wasn't worth it.

"Carla Wilson?"

"Here" my roommate shouted from her bed. The C.O moved on, keys hitting her wide hips.

"You finished your plan yet?" I knew she thought I was crazy and that's why I carefully gave her only half of my business.

"Carla don't start no shit with me today ok?"

"I'm only saying your old ass needs to get used to the idea of being here is all" Carla teased.

"I don't have to get use to shit, he's gonna come around" I barked back.

I lie down on my thin cot staring at the top of her bunk. 15 years is a long time to think about your life. I understood Raheim and what I remember most is that he was a stubborn bastard just like his father. Right when my eyes began to close I could feel Carla slide into the spot beside me covering my tits with her hand. She always knew when to make me feel better. The room felt less cold when her soft mouth cupped my nipple. I closed my eyes and remembered Carlos.

Raheim Starz

The music in the club was so loud it made the floor jump. Right away I noticed the thick cloud of smoke hanging over everybody's head like a bad news cloud. All of the wanna be ballers stood around the bar watching all the ladies on the dance floor. A tall dark skinned brotha was already eyeing me hard from the corner. "And the shit begins" I thought. I didn't see Felicia or any of her girls so I took the first available seat at a table full of honeys all rockin' knock off Gucci bags.

"Can I sit here?" I yelled over the music and not waiting for an answer I slid into the booth.

"Damn Papi, can I get your name and number?" The girl sitting directly in front of me asked. I gave her a quick once over. Her white tube top was to low and showed about sixty stretch marks crawling up her saggy tits. She had on about six $2.00 colorful plastic bangle bracelets and enough foundation to cover a small elephant. However, I'm not one to disrespect.

"I'll tell you my name if you tell me yours. " All eyes were on me all but one of her girls who was giving her the evil eye.

"My name is Simone and you can have my home #, cell number # and my mama's # if you want that too" She started giggling and her girls followed.

"Well Ms. Simone my name is Vic" I gave one of my aliases no need having her telling everybody she knows me.

"Vic? I like that."

"What yall drinking?" I asked. I didn't have a problem paying for one round of drinks. Simone quickly spoke up

"Rum and coke" I gave her a fifty-dollar bill and told her and two of her girls to get five rum and cokes leaving me at the table with the finest of the four. The one with the evil eye.

"Why you looking so mad?" She didn't say nothing for a second.

"I'm ok; it's just that my girls act so desperate sometimes." I took a card with my number on it and slid it across the table, she grabbed it and stuffed it in her purse before the giggling trio came back talking loud and dancing along to one of Beyoncé's throwbacks All The Single Ladies. No sooner than my drink hit the table Felicia's fine ass walked up. She had about twenty girls with her and they all watched the table.

"Excuse me ladies, can I borrow him for a minute?" She took me by the hand and we walked off. That's what I loved about her she didn't act out but stole the show.

"How long you been here?" she leaned her body against me until I could smell her hair. It was driving me crazy.

"Not that long" I wrapped my arms around her waist and watched the haters hate. She looked sexy as hell in a black jersey knit halter-top cat suit with a gold chain belt and matching open toe gold sandals.

"Do Beverly's old man know she in here shaking her ass?"

"I 'on know, but be quiet Raheim" She started dancing up on me moving her hips to Jamie Fox' joint blame it on the alcohol. I knew I didn't want any alcohol when I laid it on her. I started feeling the music and pulled her ass into my hardness.

Her girls surrounded us forming a circle like some shit straight from off of soul train. But just when I started feeling ok about coming to this broke down club the dark

12

skinned brotha with the eye problem stepped up in the circle with a serious attitude. He stood in front of me like he might try something. I kept dancing daring that nigga to make a move. Felicia slowed down a bit her body tensing up.

"Relax baby this muthafucka can't be that crazy" I whispered in her ear. Seconds later he grabbed her by the arm like he wanted to be smooth and tried to pull her to him but she yanked her arm away and one of her girls grabbed my arm.

"What the fuck is your problem?"

"You talking to me?" his voice had ten times the base.

"No muthafucka I'm talking to the ugly nigga behind you. Did I give your dumb ass permission to come over here and touch somebody?" I gritted on him hard and if need be I would knock his ass out. I could see a few people stop dancing and start to crowd around exactly what I didn't want.

"Nobody want that stank bitch anyway" Felicia was two seconds from swinging at his face before Beverly pulled her by the waist. "You got about two fucking minutes to back the fuck off before I whip your ugly ass." With no warning he swung his heavy fist near my face catching the bridge of my nose. I jerked back before charging at him. Hitting him with a left hook to his chin and a right to his temple. I went back to my first ass whipping my uncle Billy gave me for coming home crying after I lost a fight. I ain't ever do that again. After I had him on the floor I stood up and started kicking him in his back and shoulders. He had blood all over his ear but he was still coming for more. I could hear

Felicia screaming "Stop, Rah come on. Somebody help" That made me hit him harder until I heard his jaw crack. His eyes were closed and for a minute I thought that he was dead until I saw his chest moving up and down. When I stood up my white linen suit was covered with blood. I felt fine so I knew it had to be his. Everybody started gasping and pushing through to see who was stretched out on the floor. Dudes who heard the heat started jetting before they got there. Felicia had all of her girl's crowd around me in case the police were out front. The night air hit my face making me realize how hot it was up inside the small club. They followed me around the block until we reached my Expedition. That nigga had me trippin. She told her girls she was riding out with me and they started hugging like I was kidnapping her or something. I knew they under estimated my ability just like the sucka lying on the club floor did.

For a long while no one said anything. I headed in the direction of my downtown apartment. No other girl had the privilege of coming to my place. It was always strictly there house. The # 1 rule is if you don't have your own shit I don't fuck with you. I'm not one of these dudes only interested in the pussy. I turn welfare bitches into career broads. We pulled up to my reserved parking space. I stopped paying rent about three years ago when I first starting breaking off my landlord. She is hot as hell for a white chic. I got out the car and opened Felicia's door. She was still quiet. To tell the truth I didn't feel much like talking either. I didn't want to tell her that my right hand was starting to swell either.

When we walked in she pretended not to look around but I designed it so you had to. I had a cream wrap around couch with a pure crystal and marble coffee table. My wall mounted 52' inch television was wired with surround sound and voice activated CD player. I had 6' tall tropical plants on either side of the TV and art deco pictures on two of the walls. My dining room had a wall-to-wall tropical fish tank that gave an aquarium feel in the dark. Almost everything in my house was given to me even down to my four-poster bed with the serpent, and Adam and Eve carved on each post.

My life was easy for the most part and I had to keep it that way. Instinct kicked in and Felicia went into the kitchen filling a freezer bag with ice cubes. I heard cabinet doors open and close before she appeared in the doorway with a glass of water and the bag of ice.

"Where's your aspirin?" She asked concerned.

"I don't have any" I watched her move around and thought for a brief moment that I could get used to this. But like I said it was a brief moment. She reached into her purse and pulled out a small bottle of Motrin. She watched me swallow all three extra strength tablets before she went into the bathroom. When she came back she had a bottle of rubbing alcohol, peroxide and a few q-tips.

"So what you're my nurse now?" I put on my brave face but my hand hurt like hell. It was starting to look like Professor Klump's in the Nutty Professor.

"You know I think you're crazy right?" She stared at me with her big brown eyes.

"Why? He came at me first. This is why I don't do the club thing" I avoided stating it was because of her and her trifling ass girl Beverly that I was there in the first place.

She placed the ice pack on my hand and started swabbing my nose with peroxide.

"Play Halo by Beyoncé," I instructed and instantly the CD player searched then played one of Felicia's favorite hits. I took a moment to enjoy the serene movement of the fish swimming in the tank, the music and the beautiful woman before me. Felicia started to dance seductively in front of me.

Damn this girl is beautiful. She towered over my chair staring down at me like some type of Amazon woman. I could feel my pants getting tighter. When I looked down I remembered the blood on my clothes.

"Oh shit" I went to stand up and she pushed me back down. Her tiny fingers undid all of the buttons on my shirt when she was done she slid my shirt to the floor and eased my wife beater over my head. She undid my watch and placed it on the dining room table.

"You ever wanted to make love?" She was serious and it caught me off guard.

"What you talking about?" My eyes followed the sway of her hips and I put one had over my hardness.

"Making love? What you mean like slow fucking? Then yeah" I answered and she smiled and looked at me with sad eyes. Halo started over.

"No I mean like express your emotions, how you feel about someone through your body, through touch?" Her eyes never left mind and it was hot all of a sudden. I wanted to take a shower get the blood off of me but something told me that if I moved I'd be ruining something.

She started taking off her cat suit exposing her bare breast. Her dark nipples looked like Hershey Kisses on top of chocolate cupcakes. My dick started jumping especially when she got to her flat stomach. Her stomach was perfect; even skin tone, no blemishes or stretch marks. My dick was out of control when I saw that she wasn't wearing panties. Her pubic hair was trimmed in a perfect triangle above her pussy. It was already slick with juices. I wanted to grab her and fuck the shit out of her but instead I stood up and picked her up by the waist. She wrapped her legs around me and her arms around my shoulders. Her fingers stroked the lines of my cornrows while I used my tongue to outline her lips. When we reached my room I lay her down on the bed gently while I undid my pants. She only stared at me in a silent trance. It was in that moment that I saw something in her eyes that looked like lust or could it be love. Feeling close to an explosion I lay in between her legs pressing my chest against her pussy. I didn't care about my hand or anything else at that moment. I focused all of my energy on softly biting her stomach. I understood slow sex, I understood fucking but what she wanted me to do I haven't done before.

I don't make love not to anyone. Why? Because love is deceptive it smiles in your face while it plots on how to hurt you. I have yet to fall in love and you will never hear me say that shit to anybody. She used her fingertips to trace the outline of my face. Her romantic mood was throwing me off a bit. I didn't know if I made her hot or if she enjoyed watching me kicking another man's ass. I moved down to her pussy and blew on it to see her clit jump that shit turned me on. Moans started from her stomach and escaped from her mouth. Causing me to press my mouth against her clit. All of her juices soaked my lips before my tongue spread her open. I sucked like I was hungry. I pulled her into my mouth flicking my tongue softly until her legs started to jerk and her hands pulled my face closer into her wetness and just when I thought she might cum I moved my mouth. She arched her back gripping my white goose feathered comforter between her fingers. I put my arm around her waist using my wounded hand to lift her up as I slid inside of her inch by inch until she started sucking my ear. I knew if she felt as good as I did she was in a damn good place. Our eyes locked and for the first time in my life I looked a woman in the eyes during sex. The moment was too intense so I looked away first. Did I like Felicia? Yes, but was I in love? I didn't want to allow myself to go there. Her pussy wrapped around my dick like a fitted glove causing me to move closer to a climax with each stroke. I wouldn't be satisfied until I heard her scream…

Felicia

When Raheim broke our stare it said it all. He wasn't mine and never would be. I'm not one of these stupid chicks who runs after him because he's fine, and he is fine, and I don't walk around oblivious to the fact that he has multiple women. But when he's with me he makes me feel like I'm the only one in the room. He doesn't look at other women when I'm around and I always have his undivided attention. Just from studying Rah I know I can't be clingy it turns him off. So I make myself unavailable, I don't answer my calls every once in a while and I'm not so quick to give up the goods. We have a policy where neither of us says anything we know the other doesn't want to hear and so far it's worked but I'm beginning to feel like its backfiring. Tonight I wanted to tell Rah that I loved him. That I know it's crazy and most would say stupid but it's true. When I stared into his eyes I wanted to see if he felt the same but he looked away and I knew he didn't. I was turned off but I knew I'd have to fake an orgasm to make him move up off me. The affection I felt a moment ago faded quickly. I started moving faster and faster on his dick.

"Yeah, ohhhh right there" He started moving faster and faster until I could feel his dick stretch my pussy. I was all ready to fake it when he did the unexpected: kissing me slow and intense until I began to shake. He knew I was a sucka for a good kiss. He spoke into my cheek and the heat of his breath made me want to be closer.

"Be real with me Felicia, you said make love to you and I want to but you may have to teach me" I didn't want to cry but my eyes began to water. Not because he said his best line but because I didn't want to have to show him how to love me. If he didn't feel love I couldn't teach him. I kissed him for a long moment and moved in circles up and down his shaft. I wanted to remember our last time. I could only be his friend and I was cool with that but I couldn't handle the emotional shit that came along with loving him. He was the epitome of every woman's dream. He was universally fine, he had long money, and his crib was lavish and just being with him bumped up your status. He told me once that sometimes his looks were a blessing and a curse and I could believe that.

Every woman wanted him for a reason and most of it was for status or materialistic reasons. But me, I just wanted to love him. An hour later and he was sound asleep. I made sure his hand was wrapped tight with a ripped t-shirt and I threw his bloody linen suit into a trash bag. I was gonna burn it when I got home. I took one last look around and tried not to picture myself as his woman. The night was a little breezy especially for what I was wearing. I got my hustle on walking to the corner to look for a cab. His block was too eerie. Nothing but shadows and tall trees and lawns that looked professionally manicured in the day but gruesome and spooky at night. I tried to look straight ahead when I noticed a silver BMW riding slow beside me. When I looked over to find an old white man wearing black rimmed glasses and silvering yellow hair sitting behind the wheel I felt a little better until he asked

"How much do you charge?"

Chapter Two:
Too Close For Comfort

Raheim

Bang, Bang, Bang

The only person stupid enough to bang on my door at 12 noon on a Wednesday was my baby brother Amir. I decided to take my time until I heard the banging persist. I knew something had to be up. I swung the door open ready to snap until I saw how panicked he looked.

"Rah? You're alive"

"Yeah nigga and so is you! What the hell is your problem?"

"I just heard on the street that a crazy dude killed you" he was serious as hell and that's what made it so funny. He pushed past me and flopped on my couch.

"The sad part is that you're just hearing about it and who the fuck told you that?" My little brother is just as pretty as I am if not prettier. His body is built like a brick wall. He works out religiously and acts all health conscious. He's trying to be an actor or a reality TV star but he's a nerd and I do mean a real nerd the kind that reads dictionaries for fun. Can quote Shakespeare or tell you why the sky is blue. He's in college trying to be a meteorologist or some shit.

"You really should try to stop cursing"

"Aww nigga don't come over here in my muthafucking house telling me shit and tell those niggas on the street to get there shit right. I didn't get my ass whipped but I kicked a niggas ass"

I watched my brother's face cringe with each foul word and I enjoyed it. He always thought I was beneath him because my mom's treated him better than me and he goes to church three days a week.

"So Aunt Sadie says ya mom been writing?" I refused to claim her as my mother because moms don't hate a kid because their pops ain't shit.

"Yeah, well she's been writing you too. You should hear her out. She really is sorry," he tried to look all sincere like he really did believe her.

"Sorry for what? For kicking me out at eleven years old? Or sorry for blasting my dad's chest wide the fuck open? I'm sure she is sorry. She can't be nothing else but sorry" I threw those words at him like lava being thrown out of a mountain. His nose started flaring like he might say something. I didn't want to upset him but he was upsetting me.

"Look, what you chose to do is your business but I would rather forget about her. She hurt me real bad man and it's cool that you want to reconnect but the only mom I have is Sadie Wilson" I put my hand to my heart. Though Felicia wrapped my hand last weekend it still felt sore it wasn't broken because my fingers moved. She's been dodging my calls lately but she'd come around she always did. I glanced at my watch letting him know his time is short. In about 1 hour my phone would be blowing up with my Wednesday girl she gets off work at 1pm today. I had her change her schedule to fit mine. She said she had a surprise for me. I bet it was Michael Jordan's white autographed NC Tarheel's throwback jersey that cost $1,505. I didn't ask her for it merely suggested but she's been pulling double shifts for the past three weeks now.

"I'm about to pull out you need a ride somewhere?" I was trying hard not to be rude but if he wanted to sit and talk about his mom I wasn't in the mood.

"I'm going to see her next Wednesday" I froze what the hell was he trying to pull?

"Ok that's cool"

"I told her your coming too." I flipped. This little nigga came to test me.

"Amir, get the fuck out right now. I'm not going anywhere and I'm not sending her shit. Get your dumb ass out of my house" He wasn't budging which meant he was set on getting his ass beat. He stood up from the couch and reached into his back pocket pulling out three envelopes and dropped them on the coffee table.

"I'm praying for you Rah, I'm praying God will soften your heart" He was laying it on thick but I didn't feel like feeling guilty.

"Don't waste your time but pray that God will keep me off your ass, now get the hell out" I wanted to throw those letters out with him but I swear I wanted to know what they said more.

Right then I hated Amir for coming here and for telling her that I was coming to see her.

I forced myself to walk into the bathroom to take a quick shower. Just like clockwork my phone started ringing and if I didn't answer on the first try she would be acting crazy.

"Baby?" I could hear her talking but my mind was still on Amir and those letters.

"Yeah, who dis?" I asked rudely.

"You don't know me now?" She sounded like she wanted to play but I wasn't in the mood.

"Look don't call here with the fucking games, who the fuck is this?" See this is where my old man went wrong and it cost him his life. He needed to know when to be smooth and when to put a broad in check.

"Sheila, what's your problem?" She sounded more hurt than angry.

"Aww baby I'm sorry. My brother just gave me bad news you forgive me?" I tried to sound as sincere as I could and it worked.

"I forgive you, you ready to see me?" She sounded excited so I knew something good was coming.

"I'm always ready to see you"

"Good meet me at my house in about an hour" she hung up before I could respond but I'm on it. In the shower I tried to wash away my brother's words but I couldn't, I couldn't stop thinking about the letters on my coffee table. Why did he choose today to drop some ole crazy shit on me? I quickly threw on my clothes before grabbing the letters and stuffing them in my back pocket. I convinced myself that they really didn't matter.

Five hours and a new pair of Sean John sunglasses, fresh pair of white Jordan's and my new Michael Jordan throwback jersey later I felt like a million bucks. Sheila held out on her gift giving until after she laid it on me, black stilettos and all. I kissed her on the forehead before promising to call later tonight. I liked Sheila but she reminded me of a puppy always looking for approval and as jacked up as I am I couldn't see myself completely ruining her life too. The bulge of the letters forced me to remember what I really didn't care to that my egg donor was trying to reach out. I drove around looking for a place to park until I found a quiet spot at Fairmount Park. It was nothing but a grassy area. There were no benches or picnic tables so I sat in my car and pulled out the first envelope. It had my name on it but Amir's address.

Dear Raheim,
I know this letter is about 15 years to late but I'm sorry.
Sorry that I was caught up in my world, that I wasn't
enough for you and your brother. I'm not gonna
ask you to forgive me, not even forget but just hear my
side...

As much as I wanted to be pissed, to feed her trifling ass letters to the birds I kept reading. She went on to explain how my pops promised to take care of us. That he said he was coming to take me and Amir shopping and when he didn't show up she was so pissed that he kept promising us shit that when she saw my face and couldn't stop seeing his she was scared she might hurt me. That was the day she kicked me out. She wanted me back but Aunt Sadie wasn't tryna hear that shit and the night she shot him was right after he promised to take me to church.

When she called my aunt's house and my aunt Sadie said he never came home that was the last straw. She took her father's shotgun out of his gun case and went looking for him. When she saw his silver Volvo parked in front of her rival's house the same Volvo that she co-signed for she shot the door down. They had the music so loud they didn't hear it. When she kicked the bedroom door in all she could see was the Italian broad riding him into the sunset. She said that didn't make her pull the trigger. It was after my pops spotted her and started laughing like he knew she was a punk. That set her off before she knew it her finger pressed the trigger and the impact blasted his chest wide open. The Italian broad was all out of laughs by then. She started scrambling to get away. My mom didn't want to kill her just make her pay so she blew both her legs off leaving her in a wheelchair for life. I didn't want to cry but the tears slid down my face involuntarily. I never thought to look at things through my mom's eyes. My father was an ass but it still didn't change what happened there were plenty of single mom's in the world that didn't kill their baby daddies but then again there were a lot that had. I decided I had enough emotion for the day so I put the letters away and sat for a while. I would never understand that kind of love that would make a man and woman go that crazy. I knew one thing was for sure I would never be like either of them. I was satisfied being in love with myself.

My phone started to ring. The number on the caller ID said it was my old Tuesday Kelly. I didn't come to see her yesterday or for the last few weeks before that and she's been blowing my phone up ever since. I answered on the fourth ring.

"Yeah?"

"Raheim?" She sounded shocked that I answered.

"Yessss, who's this?" I knew that would piss her off.

"It's Kelly why you didn't come over yesterday?" She was suppressing her irritation.

"Because I was busy, why you miss me?

"You know I do" her voice softened a bit.

"Oh ok, why you calling me anyway? You told me not to come back remember?"

"Raheim stop playing"

"That's just it baby girl. I'm not playing. You have too many damn mood swings and I don't have time for that shit. Why you not at work anyway?"

"Because I wanted to make up from last week"

"So you call out of work?" That alone was enough for a cut. I didn't roll with slackers you were either up on your game or you weren't. That reminded me of today's engagement in Atlantic City. I had two of the finest chic's working on my business.

"Kelly I'm gonna put it to you like this. I liked you, a lot but I don't think I can provide you with what you're looking for"

"Don't try to feed me with the bullshit Raheim. You probably fuckin somebody right now. One of these days your damn dick gonna fall off!" I couldn't help but laugh. I swear the redbones are the craziest.

"Time is money so later"

"Wait" she screamed before I could flip my phone shut.

"I don't care what you say you're mine. I love you boo and I'm sorry for acting a little off but I have a lot of shit going on right now. Stuff you don't even know about. Let me prove it to you just come over and I'll do it to you better than anybody else. You know you want it"

"I'm gonna pass. Take care of yourself Kelly" I flipped my phone shut I'm convinced that her ass is bipolar. I would need to run home for a quick shower and change of clothes. I had to meet up with Alexis and Maya at the Trump Taj Mahal by 10pm. These broads were the best in the business. I met Maya first about two years ago when I was on one of my regular trips to AC. It was cold as hell and I was donning my waist length black and white chinchilla jacket, True Religion jeans and my new black leather Timberlands. I had just come in and sat at the bar when I was approached by Maya a tall, curly head slender honey. She wasn't my initial type but she had on a slinky black dress with 4-inch heels so I made an exception. She stroked my jacket a few times and I knew she was gaming when she started whispering that sexy shit in my ear. I stood up and walked away, I never let any broad think I was pressed save that for the tricks or the bum dudes. Like I expected she was walking behind me.

"Oh, I'm sorry that wasn't an invitation." I left her standing there speechless. She spotted me again at the high roller machines and outright asked.

"Are you gay?" It was hard not to laugh. It was so easy to knock a woman off her square.

"No, I'm just not into prostitutes" 'I knew my words would sting and I intended for them to. After several minutes of silence she started to cry not actual boo hooing but a few tears.

"You're an asshole"

"Actually I'm not, what I said was true I'm not into prostitutes and I know a woman as fine as you don't need to be hustling these streets."

"Who are you Jesus' side kick?" She snapped back with a signature don't judge me stare.

"No far from it. All I'm saying is that while you're out here taking the streets money is being lost."

"I don't want a pimp. The only person getting paid from my pussy is me" I didn't want to tell her that what she was getting was far less than what was taken from her.

"Fair enough but I'm not a pimp just a dude who gone take you upscale." That was the beginning of a beautiful working relationship. I turned her on to my corporate connects who was willing to pay $5,000 a week to see her pretty ass. These dudes weren't bum dudes either I'm talking suckas who made six figure incomes and rode around in Ferrari's and Rolls Royce's. Took vacations in the Hamptons. I met these connects through a few of my female associates and I presented the deal they didn't want to refuse.

Eventually Maya recruited her girl Alexis and they gave me 25% at the end of every week. I took these broads from $1,200 a week to $40,000. My profit is $20,000 a week off of their combined $80,000. Shit couldn't be sweeter. They both knew somebody who wanted to be down but I was only interested in them for now. Too many broads get on board and the heat might come down on me. I let the two girls I had before them go when they started complaining about my cut. Life is too short for the bullshit.

Janet Starz

It was twenty minutes before head count and I just came back to my cell. There was no mail waiting for me yet again. I was expecting to hear back from Amir by now. I gave him the letters I wanted him to give to Raheim over a week ago and I still didn't know if he did it or not. I knew if I could get Raheim on my side he could pay a few top-notch lawyers to look over my case. A few of the girls in the same block told me that his paper is stacked long. I wasn't impatient I could wait. It's just that it was taking longer than I expected. I had a visit later with my mom and my aunt. My dad disowned me the night Carlos was killed. He claimed I deserved what Carlos did nagging him the way I did. What type of shit was that to say? I only nagged because my sons were going without and I would be damned if I was gonna allow that nigga to live it up while we were struggling. I took a minute to look at the picture of Amir taped to the gray concrete wall above my metal desk. He was all grown up and fine as hell, a model type. I couldn't allow myself to feel too many emotions or it would make me go crazy.

My roomie was having one of her down days so I tried to stay out of her way. I fought back the urge to feel sorry for myself. My mom hated seeing me look sad so I put on my happy face and pretended shit was good but the reality is I'm 45 years old in prison for life with a son who hates me and the only man I ever loved dead by my hand. I watched the C.O walk with her clipboard checking off names until she reached our cell. We both gave a quick here to get it over with. I took this time to clean up for my visit slicking my hair back with water as neatly as I could. I stood over the metal sink trying to be as quiet as possible. Pretending I couldn't hear Carla sniffling into her pillow. I needed my eyebrows done which made me remember how fly I was on the streets.

That's how Carlos kept me until I got pregnant. I was the envy of every race of woman. He was sexy as hell. His tall athletic frame forced you to look up at him and his strong arms fit perfectly around my waist. He was so gorgeous I found it hard to resist and then harder to let go. I knew he was all wrong for me but I didn't care especially after my sons got here and his pretty ass thought it was too easy to walk away. His attitude drove me crazy riding around in the car with my name on it with that bitch Gianni. The sight of the two of them naked and laughing at me like I was a joke tipped me completely over the edge. I wanted to kill her too but I wanted her to suffer more. Out of everything that happened that night the only thing I don't regret was blowing Gianni's legs off. She would always remember not to mess with what was mine and that was well worth my ride in hell.

Raheim Starz

It was no trouble getting to my regal suite at the Trump Taj Mahal. Mr. Trump knew how to do it big. The large marble foyer greeted me when I slid my key card in the door. The cream walls were enhanced by gold awnings and baseboards. A quiet fire blazed in the fireplace letting me know the girls were already here. Although I couldn't see them the pieces of their clothing coming from the direction of the bedroom told me where they were. The sliding doors were open in the bedroom so I took a walk to the doorway only to find Maya and Alexis lying on the perfectly made king size bed naked. Alexis' slightly darker skin shimmered with body glitter as she lie on her back legs spread wide while Maya lay at Alexis's side stroking her tits as a way to entice me. See, though I am a freak I am a businessman first. I have never slept or intend to give it to either of them no matter how much my dick may jump.

"Are we having a party I didn't know about?" I dropped my key card on the table beside the door. Alexis deliberately slid a finger in her pussy making it shiny with her juices and used it to call me closer. I chose to use restraint instead and walked out of the room to the bar. I remembered one of the lessons my boy Dre taught me he said that a true playa learns how to control his dick. Though a woman's pussy is powerful it ain't shit without a man's dick.

"Get dressed both of you" I gave them time to meet me in the living room wrapped up in their robes before I opened a bottle of Moet.

"We have a few things to go over. I have two new clients who want in which will bring you both up to $45,000 apiece. The question is can either of you handle it?" Maya's face look interested. She was hooked to the money but Alexis looked like the business was starting to get to her.

"I'm in, who couldn't use another five grand? Long as he's not like crazy ass Mr. Torini I can't take another one of his crazy ass humiliation games" Maya commented making Alexis laugh and add her two cents.

"Or Mr. Boyer's weird ass diaper changes. All the money these dudes make just to be into some weird freak shit" The two girls started laughing but I didn't see shit funny. The weird freak shit is what took them from being common street whores to upscale escorts.

"I didn't know there was a problem. How about we find two new chicks from the streets who would appreciate the hands that feed them" They both stopped laughing.

"Damn Raheim you need to stop being so uptight" Maya rolled her eyes at me.

"I understand these dudes are really fucked up in the head. Too much power and it starts messing with you but you agreed to the shit. Now Alexis if you want a tradeoff let me know now. We can drop old dude and start with my new connect, same money" I watched her expression thinking it over. She was pretty, a little weathered but still pretty. I tried not to wonder why she was on the streets, what or who led her there because like I always say business is business.

"I'll keep Mr. Boyer" She didn't think I knew about the big tips he left her for a job well done. I wanted to ask her what she was complaining for then but I downed a glass of Moet instead.

Chapter Three:
Don't Mess Wit My Paper

I first got the call about my baby daddy from his boy Ray saying he was in the hospital. I tried not to show emotion on the plane back from Atlanta but with Drake down my financial security was uncertain. I was pissed when Ray called me knowing I was on vacation at my mom's place in 'Hotlanta' where the sun goes to play and the bruthas are a plenty. My heart nearly dropped when he said the words no woman ever wants to hear about her man. "You need to come to the hospital"

Ten hours later and I was walking into the Univ. of Penn through the gates building off of Spruce Street. The nurse sitting behind the desk looked fairly young with blonde hair pulled into a ponytail. Her blue nurse's uniform shirt fit loosely around her tall frame.

"I'm looking for Drake Pendergrass, I'm his wife" I wasn't his wife yet but she didn't need to know my business.

"He is in room" she paused to take a look at the clipboard sitting in front of her "102, here take this visitors pass and sign your name right here" I took the pass after signing my name and headed toward the elevators. When I got close to room 102 I didn't know what I expected to see but what greeted me behind the doors made me want to scream. Drake was lying motionless in a hospital bed. It was elevated upright with wires connected to a machine. Metal rods were surrounding his head like a halo and two of the rods were bolted to either side of his jaw. He couldn't turn to see me enter but his eyes weren't open anyway. They were swollen shut and black and blue. It looked like he went toe to toe with a tractor-trailer and lost.

I tried to talk to Drake but what could I say? I whispered in his ear that I was here and that I loved him. I didn't know if he could hear me or not but I kept talking anyway. Twenty minutes later and his eyes started to flutter half way open. I knew he was happy to see me because he squeezed my hand but his mouth was wired shut so he couldn't talk to me. I didn't need to hear him speak to know what he wanted to say. I was a real ass bitch that would ride or die for my paper but I cried when I saw a tear escape his eyelid and slide down to his hospital gown.

Ray only gave me half of the story but told me that a pretty nigga was to blame. He wasn't with Drake that night so he could only go off the word of a few club goers there that night. He asked me if I wanted him and a few of his boys to handle it but I told him no. That nigga is gonna learn that when you fuck with me or my money that there would be hell to pay. If I couldn't do the job then I'd call on the big dogs but until then I was gonna handle my business my way.

Platinum Dust

Raheim

It was Friday and Felicia still not answering her line. To be honest the shit was driving me crazy. I hadn't seen her for three weeks now and my boy Dre said he saw her at the movies last Saturday. Just when I wanted to call her again my cell rang. I didn't recognize the number so it went unanswered until it rang again with the same number.

"Hello?"

"May I speak to Vic?" the voice sounded too young to be calling me.

"Who's this?"

"It's Tamia, remember the girl from the club?" she tried to help me remember but I swear at the moment I couldn't.

"What club?"

"Six-Nine, I was with my friends and you slid your card to me"

"Oh, oh I remember now. Why you take so long to call me?" I put on my best playboy voice.

"Why are you busy?" She had an innocent tone, which I kinda liked.

"No what's up, everything good?"

After talking for about twenty minutes I learned that she was only twenty-three, which explained her voice, she had her own apartment and was in her senior year at Temple University. I was sitting in my truck on my way to check her out with my mind on Felicia. I had to shake it off because you can't dwell on shit for too long. In my rearview I spotted the same silver Infinity trailing one car behind for

37

the past ten blocks. I hung a sharp right confident I lost them. I knew I didn't owe anybody unlike Dre the city's biggest heroin and coke dealer. He had connections from here to Mexico and everywhere in between. He had the occasional sucka looking for him but I never got caught up in his transactions. The darkness concealed the numbers on the apartment door so it was difficult to see which one was hers so I had to park. Tamia was waiting for me on the steps, which took me by surprise. I quickly snapped back when I spotted the skin tight Ed Hardy jeans and a teal spaghetti strap Fendi shirt. Her ass looked good so I walked behind her a step to get a good look.

We hopped in the Expedition and I sped off. Shorty had a good conversation piece too, which let me know she was on her 'A' game. Three blocks later I couldn't help but notice the same silver Infinity. I told Tamia to hold on before weaving in and out of traffic through semi busy streets. I dodged a few cars and ran a red light with the car still on my heels.

"What is wrong with you?" she yelled at me with the signature black woman head roll.

"I'm cool, why you ask?" I didn't know who it was and Kelly drove a blue Camry so I knew it wasn't her crazy ass. Tamia turned in her seat to look out the back window before screaming at the top of her lungs.

"Vic? Vic" She slapped my arm a few times to get my attention but I couldn't turn around or we'd both be dead.

"VIC" Her voice boomed through my truck.

"WHAT?" I shouted back, she had me paranoid.

"LOOK" Tamia grabbed the wheel turning it left into a dark alley. Right when I wanted to ask if she had lost her mind the back window of the Expedition shattered.

"Oh shit" Tamia started screaming and tryna open her car door.

"Relax, give me a minute to think" The car was coming at me faster and it was a dead end ahead. I know I wasn't about to die on some ole crazy gangsta shit.

"Listen Tamia, I need you to grab my piece from the glove compartment. I'm gonna hit reverse aim at the window when I say three" My voice was as relaxed as it was gonna get under the circumstances.

"I don't want to. Just take me home please. Oh God please." Tears were streaming down her face like an open faucet. I knew this broad wasn't bout it and now I was caught slipping. I started yelling hoping I put the fear of God in her.

"Listen to me NOW. When I say three you're gonna aim that muthafucking gun at that muthafucka. Do you hear me? Do YOU?" She looked at me with big eyes but she reached in the glove compartment pulling out my 9mm. Just seeing my piece put me at ease, this broad was starting to get on my nerves she was practically hyperventilating. Her hand shook uncontrollably. I hit the gas and my truck reeled backward at top speed.

"When I say three blast that window ok?" She only nodded her head. "One...Two...Three" I only heard one shot going off and then glass shattering. The infinity was trying to back out of the alleyway but their skills weren't as good as mine. I front ended their car trying to get a good look at the driver. I couldn't make out the facial features but the silhouette told me it was a woman with wild, curly hair. When she finally spun out of the alley I followed behind. The hunted becoming the hunter.

"Now what Bitch?" I was in a zone until Tamia's voice broke in.

"Please take me home. Now please" I looked over at her and felt sorry for having her in the middle of this craziness. She was too young to be in my world anyway. Her mascara was running and her hair sweated out.

"Alright, relax, you hungry?" Her head snapped in my direction letting me know she thought I was crazy. I called Book Binders from my cell ordering shrimp scampi, mussels Alfredo and clam chowder. I was familiar with the chef. I tried to calm down before swinging over to pick up my food. All I could think of was that I needed to know who was out to get me and fast.

*** Felicia***

Yeah I saw how many times Rah tried to call but he needs to sweat. I've been making myself busy trying to get a life outside of him. After the whole club scene I've been reevaluating myself. My girl Beverly calls me every five minutes talking about her wedding plans and while I'm trying to be happy for her I'm sad for myself. I've been spotting for almost two weeks now, my boobs are sore and my period is three weeks late. I'm denying the inevitable and I'm trying not to go to the Dr's for another week or so to find out what I already know.

I can't tell none of my girls because they are only gonna tell me to tell Raheim and that I wouldn't do. I already feel stupid as it is and I know how much he ain't tryna have no kids. This would be my burden and I'm damn sure not gonna let it drive me to do what his crazy ass mama did. I was tired of staying in and though my Fridays have been spent with Raheim I've been doing pretty good switching up my routine. I called my girl Coco, nicknamed after Coco Chanel cause all she wore was Chanel everything.

"You up for going out?"

"You know it, what club we hittin up? I just got my hair done" She was a club hopping queen. She loved the scene, the vibe and the hustlers. She stayed getting her hair and nails done just to show it all off on the weekend.

"I don't feel like going to a club tonight" I whined.

"Hold up, ain't it Friday? Why you not with Raheim. Let me find out you stepping out and I will kick your skinny ass myself"

"Shut up, nobody is stepping out and he's not my man anyway" I tried to convince myself more than her.

"Keep telling yourself that shit if you want to but Rah ain't leaving you alone" Her words were meant to make me feel better but it only hurt thinking that my little secret was the kryptonite that could keep him away for good.

"Come on Chanel let's go out to eat"

"I can eat at home, I wanna get my dance on" I knew she was imitating a dance as she talked

"Well see you then. Get your nasty on and call me later" After hanging up I put on my jeans and a Bob Marley t-shirt. I felt like Chinese, so I would walk over to my favorite take out spot.

52nd street strip was still busy and it was ten thirty. The bums were rummaging through the overflowing trashcans on each corner. Groups of wanna be taxi's stood under the EL terminal shouting "Hack man, Hack man, anybody need a hack" Girls dressed in their best knock offs looking for a come up dude walked to the corner stores for no reason. I walked pass the bright lights of Crown Chicken and into my favorite Chinese store with the graffiti laced walls and bulletproof glass window. There was a group of teenage boys, each sportin' skinny jeans hanging off their ass revealing dusty boxers.

"Yo gimme a Dutch" the tallest of the group tapped the glass disrespectfully.

"Right there muthafucka" I hated when they did that making me swear to kick my kids behind if they acted like that. His buddies started laughing as they left the store.

Ten minutes later my food was ready. I picked up my pace walking faster to my house then I had to the store. Turning down Cedar Ave I could have sworn I just saw Rah's Expedition turn the corner but the back window was shattered. I just knew I had to be mistaken.

Platinum Dust

Raheim

I dropped Tamia off at her apartment with her food and a few dollars for tonight's trouble. I needed to be with someone that could calm me down. I tried Felicia again and this time she answered.

"Hello?"

"Felicia, I need to see you now. Open your door." I flipped my phone not giving her a chance to tell me no. I needed to call Dre see if he heard anything on the streets. Felicia's door was unlocked when I got there. All the lights were out; the haze of the TV was the only thing that lit the room.

"You ok?" I had to ask cause this was not like what I expected. Her hair was up in a messy ponytail, she had on the sweatpants she only wore when she cleaned up and there were open Chinese food containers on the coffee table.

"Yeah are you? Is that your truck with the busted windows?" she didn't look at me when she talked.

"How you know about that?" I stood over her.

"I saw you driving when I went to the store." She still didn't look at me.

"Why you not looking at me?" I had to get to the bottom of this.

"And why you stop answering my calls?" I dropped down beside her on the couch.

"Stop acting like you noticed. Don't worry Rah I know my place. It's on Friday's"

"Yo, you alright Felicia? What the fuck is your problem huh? You sitting up in here in the dark like you crazy and shit and you dropped me. Don't forget that part" Tonight was getting crazier by the minute my best girl was changing up and I was this close to being dead.

"I need space Raheim, I am going crazy, I'm tired of pretending I don't care, when I do" she was crying and I felt like I entered into the twilight zone.

"Felicia, I need you to listen to me. I was chased tonight, somebody shot at my car that's why the window is broke. I don't know who it was. Yo, the shit is crazy. I need you to let me use your phone." Even in the dark her eyes were unmistakable. She looked at me with pure anger and before I knew what was happening she jumped up from the couch and darted toward the window.

"WHAT?"

"Exactly, somebody is tryna take me out. Now listen I need to call Dre" she cut me off.

"I need you to leave"

"What? You trippin" she looked serious and it made my dick hard. She was pretty when she was mad.

"Raheim please. I can't risk this. Not right now. I know you don't understand but I can't have this type of drama" Before I could answer she was at the door holding it open for me. Shit was getting deep. I didn't argue but it hurt I refused to let her see it though. I left out reaching for my cell.

"Hey Dre?"

"Where you been?" I could hear his music in the background.

"Hangin, listen I had some serious shit go down tonight, where you at?" I looked around her block before I stepped in my car.

"I'm over on Woodland meet me here in 30. Be safe and stop messing over all those broads?'

"Shut up, alright man see you" I knew Dre could handle my business we've been friends since 11 years old and he was always a bad ass. He started hustling the day after his thirteenth birthday when his pops rolled out leaving his mom to face an eviction notice on her own. He never looked back and his mom ain't ever want for nothing since. I navigated the streets of Southwest Philly watching my mirrors for any sign of a silver Infinity.

Dre's spot looked like a typical house in the hood. Front lawn littered with trash, dull and chipped gray paint on the porch railings and the windows donning newspaper curtains. I knocked twice wondering if he could hear me over the music coming from the inside. I could see movement behind the window before hearing a female voice

"Who is it?"

"It's Raheim for Dre" The latch on the door clicked and the door eased open revealing a barely dressed beauty. Her skin was the color of cinnamon. She was topless but her most valuable asset was covered by a pink thong. She turned to get my man for me. My eyes were glued to her perfectly shaped ass as she switched extra hard knowing I was watching. Dre came from the empty dining room. He had a new scar lining the whole right side of his face.

"Hey playboy"

"What up?" We did our signature handshake pulling one another in for a semi hug. I started spilling out the night's events in full animation.

"Sounds to me like you have yourself a problem; let me finish up with this business and I'll get wit you. Sit up in the back room" He motioned with two fingers for Ms. Cinnamon to show me up.

"Candy treat my boy right." My eyes followed her ass all the way to the top. We walked by three doors to get to the back room. It looked like the cracked paint was scratched by tiger claws. She used a key to let us in. A queen size bed was against the wall covered with a black satin comforter and red satin and lace pillows it sat across from the windows. A tall bamboo chest of drawers was the home of numerous lit candles and a clear bowl with floating tea lights. I sat on the chair in the corner taking in the contours of her breast, the arch in her back and the swell of her hips.

"What's your name?" she slowly unpinned her hair so it fell around her face.

"Raheim" after all of the stress from tonight I welcomed this change.

"Here" she sauntered over handing me one of those new Raw Dawg condoms that promised to make it feel dangerously close to not having one on. The wrapper promised it would feel like I was ridin raw. She dipped to her knees in front of me pulling her hair over one shoulder. I didn't have time to ask questions before my pants were unzipped and my hardness all nine and half inches were consumed. Her tongue performed magic moving in rhythmic circles and then up and down my shaft. Her soft hand followed the beat of her lips she was taking me there bringing me closer and closer to the edge. When I felt like releasing my seed and the veins in my dick started to throb she stopped. I wanted to grab her by the back of her head and hold her there but I didn't. Within seconds she towered over me rolling the condom down like a professional. Then she placed one foot on the arm of the chair in a backwards cowboy. She slammed down on my rod like her life depended on it. Home girl was going for broke. I grabbed her by the waist and rocked her ass.

Seconds later she started to moan.

"Oh hell no mami" I pulled her off my lap and stood up ready for doggie but she flipped the script on me turning to bite my shoulder. I wasn't tryna get bruises. So I pushed her back on the bed catching a glimpse of fire in her eyes.

"Fuck me" I went to grab her waist but she moved and shouted "I said fuck me" she came at me ready to bite again. I grabbed her by her wrist and swung her against the wall. Shorty liked it rough but I wasn't with this shit; I was too hot to stop. She held me by the back of my neck wrapping her legs around my waist. The wall was our anchor as I thrust my dick in and out of her so hard I felt her uterus move.

"Fuck me" she started screaming eyes rolling in the back of her head.

"I said fuck me Muthafucka" I could feel the buildup rushing to my swollen head ready to explode while she bounced up and down on it. I tried not to lose my balance but my pants pooled around my ankles making it difficult.

"Harder, Harder" She kept moving until I went limp and slid out of her wetness. She surprised me by sliding the condom carefully from my manhood and dropping it into the trashcan beside the chair before licking her lips and walking out. About ten minutes later my boy Dre came in smiling.

"Candy is the truth isn't she?" all I could do was shake my head. That would be the last time I let him recommend anyone.

"Alright playboy, run it by me again" Dre said a bit more serious.

"A silver Infinity ran me down and shot out my back window. I'on know who the fuck it was but I need to find out like yesterday."

"I just made a few calls to the boys on the block and Reese told me that a chic name Shante was heard saying you need to watch your back"

"Shante? Who is that?"

"I'on know nigga but what I do know is that you need to narrow your list of hoes down to about ten" He laughed like the shit was funny.

"Dre, do you see my face? Does it look like I'm fucking laughing to you right now?"

"You right" he put his game face on.

"Look, from now on until you know who after your ass stay discreet. Don't give no new broads your number and rent a new car nothing flashy, keep it simple. I'll ask around some more and get back at you tomorrow. Meet me here around three." I couldn't stop looking at the scar on his face it was still open revealing pink flesh which was a noticeable contrast to his dark skin. Reading my thoughts he explained.

"I had a run in with Ronnie two weeks ago. That nigga tried to rob a few of my runners over on 60th street. I had to handle it. He got a few hits off with the butt of his gun." He traced the scar with his fingertips.

"Who little ass Ronnie?" I was seriously shocked last time I saw Ronnie he was riding a big wheel on the block.

"He ain't little no more but anyway you don't have to worry about his ass no more I put him and his crew to sleep." For a minute I felt sorry for Ronnie he used to be a good kid.

"You want to stay here tonight?" He stood up to leave.

"Naw, I'm good but thanks man"

"Alright then my brotha but open the windows up in this bitch" He threw his head back and laughed all the way outta the room. Dre only relaxed around me I was like his brother, his only brother. I finished getting dressed and headed back downstairs avoiding Candy as I hit the door. A group of Dre's front men escorted me to my truck.

"Yo they fucked ya shit up. You know who did it?" the one they call little man remarked. He got his nickname because he was short and always had on clothes three sizes too big. Like tonight his army pants pooled at his feet covering his shoes and his white t-shirt nearly swallowed him. He looked like a kid playing dress up. I didn't need to answer because Chuck the taller of the two stepped in.

"Man shut up. If he knew you think he would be taking it up with Dre?" He rolled his eyes and I ignored them both hopping in my ride, pissed that my window was busted. Back at my crib my voicemail light was blinking on the cordless. I didn't have the energy to answer not after tonight. Just when my eyes started feeling heavy my car alarm started blazing. I jumped up running out the apartment taking the stairs two at a time. Where the fuck is the cops when you really need them? I asked myself. All I saw was the back end of the silver Infinity screeching around the corner. I ran up to my truck to find that all my windows were busted out. Shattered glass was on the front and back seats and on the ground surrounding my tires. A note was left on the driver's seat.

You fucked with the wrong bitch. I'm coming after your ass until I see blood.

The words sent goose bumps up my arms. I would have to go see Kelly because if it was her crazy ass I swear I would kill her. I figured most of the damage was done for the night but I knew sleep was out of the question. Knowing someone wanted to kill me eliminated any desire to rest even if my bed was soft as clouds. I ran over the last few weeks in my head and couldn't think of any girl other than Kelly who would be upset enough to come at me.

I had to know if she was behind tonight's nonsense so I picked up my cell and dialed her number from contacts. She answered on the first ring.

"Hello." She sounded like I just woke her up.

"Yo Kelly? Where were you tonight?" I asked trying not to sound to hype.

"Who dis?" Now really wasn't the time to play dumb.

"Raheim, how many niggas are you fuckin wit?" I could hear her moving the covers around to sit up.

"None you just woke me up. I'm home. How you gone call me asking questions when yo ass haven't been answering none of mine?"

"Did you go out earlier?"

"No I stayed in and watched a few movies. Why?"

"Cause I thought I saw you in a silver Infinity an hour ago." I played it off in case it wasn't her.

"Raheim stop playing wit me you already know what kind of car I drive. Why would I be in an Infinity? Any way you acting like you miss me boo I can buzz you in the building if you want to slide on through real quick." I was half tempted by her offer because it was too dangerous to stay here in my crib alone. But I really didn't feel like dealing with Kelly's crazy ass tonight. I couldn't even fake it good enough to try.

"Maybe next time, I'm a bit busy tonight.

"Please don't be playing me Raheim, I really do miss you and I have an itch only you can scratch." The one thing about Kelly is that she knew how to stroke my ego.

"I'm not playing I'm gonna hit you later ok?"

"Alright sexy, talk to you." I hung up before she could say anything else. With no desire to sleep I went into my bedroom and started searching for important papers to put into my black Louis Vuitton bag. I wouldn't be sleeping here tonight knowing Infinity knew I was here. I would have to stay at a hotel until I could figure out my next move

.

Chapter Four:
Things Get Heated

Raheim Starz

Having to look over my shoulder all the time was getting old real fast as I weaved through busy Saturday afternoon traffic in my rented Nissan Altima. Searching through the streets for a silver Infinity, as I headed over to my boy Dre's spot on Woodland Ave, made me feel off my game.

I hit up Dre before I parked so I wouldn't have to spend time on the porch. Before I could lift my hand to the door, crazy ass Candy was there holding it open.

"Hey sexy," she smiled at me like I was something good to eat.

"Hey, where Dre?" I walked by her, being sure not to touch her, on my way in.

"He's upstairs; you need another red light Candy special?" Her words meant nothing to me at this point.

"No thanks, my arm is still fucked up where you bit me." I headed for the staircase, not turning to see her rolling her eyes. Chuck stood at the top of the stairs with his Glock 23 clearly visible under his shirt.

53

"Dre waiting for you in the back," he said as he nodded his head in the direction of the back room. I guess he was supposed to be security.

I tapped on the door twice before opening. It was like entering into a man cave/security booth. He had about ten 13-inch TV's filling the walls, feeding him images of each section of the house. There was one 52' inch TV resting in a large entertainment center, blasting a college basketball game. Dre sat in a black lay Z boy with his feet propped up.

"Hey Rah, I was just talking to my man's about you," Dre never took his eyes off the game.

"Well what did he have to say?"

"He said the streets wasn't talking, he hadn't heard anything, but would keep an eye out," came his apologetic tone over his shoulder.

I couldn't believe I would have to walk around paranoid until someone found out something.

"You sure it's not one of those chicken heads you screwed around with?" Dre continued, "I keep telling you to stop fucking with fifty broads. Keep one ride or die and you have only one problem."

Maybe he was right. Having to many women to keep track of was a hassle. You never knew if two or more of them knew each other. If one of them saw me out with someone else, they could've pitched a fit, leaving me windowless. Whoever it was, I knew I'd have to find her and fast.

Platinum Dust

Felicia

It'd been a few days since I'd last seen Raheim. I felt
bad for kicking him out but I couldn't have him bringing all
of his girl drama to my house right now. I especially didn't
feel like hearing about another damned woman being
scorned. After work I stopped to pick up a pregnancy test,
regretting that decision as I stood in front of my bathroom
doorway. The lump in my throat wouldn't go away no
matter how hard I swallowed. It was now or never. I hyped
myself up to pee on the stick that would determine my fate.
If it came back negative I would go out for a drink, but if it
came back positive I would most likely find myself passed
out on the bathroom floor. I closed my eyes and counted to
three, refusing to look at the stick until after I changed my
clothes and ate dinner. I tried hard to swallow my baked
chicken and mashed potatoes from last night's leftovers.

"Why are you tripping? You're not pregnant and you're
gassing your head up for nothing?" I spoke aloud to myself,
thinking maybe if I heard the words, it would somehow
make them true. When I couldn't pretend any longer, I did a
slow death walk to the bathroom. The white stick sat on the
sink, daring me to look. Before I could find an excuse to run
out of that bathroom, I lifted the stick to see the pink
positive sign glaring back at me. I was pregnant and it was
final. No more guessing, pretending or ignoring the fact that
my stomach was getting tighter and my breasts were getting
larger.

K.C Blaze

"Shit!!!" I screamed to no one and everyone. I wanted to be happy, I wanted to act like I was going to be ok, doing everything on my own, but most importantly, I wanted to cry for being so damned stupid.

Janet Starz

I tried to find a quiet place to read the letter Amir had just sent. My cellmate was talking with a group of girls in our room, so that was out of the question. I found an empty chair in the library and looked around before taking a seat. There were a few shady bitches in here that hated the idea of someone else getting mail. I was happy to see that he put a few dollars on my commissary, so I wouldn't have to worry this month like the rest of these broads. In his letter, Amir said he gave my letters to Raheim and that he wasn't that thrilled to receive them. I knew that much, his ass was just like his dad, so it would take a moment for him to come around. I tried not to cry when I read that he was praying for me. Sons aren't supposed to pray for their mamas.

I would do anything to go home again. Even kiss Raheim's spoiled ass until he helped out. Amir was loyal and that's why I had a soft spot for him. I couldn't help but favor him; especially with how much attention he gave me when I was first sentenced to this hellhole. He wrote me letters and sent me his allowance money. I had to tell him to be careful not to let Sadie know what he was doing or she'd put an instant stop to it.

Sadie ran a tight ship and wouldn't even let my mom and dad see the boys for almost four years, until my mom went around to her house crying in the streets saying she was sorry for what I did. Carlos was her baby brother and she never liked me from jump, but I didn't care. For a moment, I was the hottest bitch on the block. I had the best clothes, the finest dude and rode in the hottest cars. Carlos gave me everything— until I gave him his kids. Then I was nobody, a toy to be played with on a whim, and thrown away when he was done.

Well not me, I had to teach him that I wasn't a joke and that he couldn't play around with my kids like that. Where was Sadie when her brother was promising to come and visit the boys? Where was she when he said he didn't care if we had food to eat? His pretty ass needed someone to give him a wakeup call and I was just the one to do it.

I eased out of my chair and walked back to my cell. There were about five chicks standing around talking about who was visiting who next week. I had better things to think about, like getting out of here before I went crazy. I didn't pretend to like any of my cellmate's friends; they were all back stabbers and loved drama, real or imagined. I walked over to my small metal desk and picked up my notebook and pencil.

"What? You don't speak?" It was always the same brown-skinned chick with a short kinky Afro that had to comment.

"My lips ain't move did they?" She was too young to be on my level and I knew she was itching to get a name for herself. What she didn't know was that I already branded myself and everyone else in here knew it. I didn't back down from nobody and I damn sure didn't show anybody fear.

"Hey Nikki, chill I don't feel like the heat coming in here today," Carla calmed her girl down and I left the small room to head back to the library. Being behind bars turned many a weak mind into animals. Only the strong survive and I was going to make sure I was the last one standing.

Raheim Starz

When I got home I didn't check my messages, even though my phone was blinking. I had already left a message with my landlord letting her know I was considering moving out. Whoever was after me knew where I lived, which was unacceptable to say the least. I needed to get away and fast. Before I could change my mind I picked up my phone and called Felicia's number. It rang five times before I heard her voice on the other end. Without thinking I closed my eyes at the sound of her voice. With all of this crazy shit happening around me, she was the only person I knew who made me see clearly.

"Hey Felicia, I need to ask you a question."

"Raheim? You're the only person I know who calls to ask questions after not speaking for weeks," she snapped, sounding happy like she had a smile on her face.

"Well, you abandoned me remember? I'm still back at the last night we spent together," I told her and she became quiet almost like she hit the mute button.

"Felicia, why you switching shit up on me? You've been ducking and weaving for over a month and a half now. Avoiding the hell outta me and I want to know why?"

"Raheim I know that's not what you called here for? I've been busy and we're not in a relationship. Sorry if I broke the mold, if I want more than what the hell you tryna give."

"What I'm tryna give? Yo where is all of this coming from? Am I in the fucking twilight zone or some shit?" I couldn't believe I was calling to ask her to take a trip and as crazy as she was acting I was tempted to change my mind, but I wanted to see her.

"You're right, we're not in a relationship and I'm sorry for coming at you all crazy, but that's not why I'm calling. I wanted to know if you would be up for a trip to Jamaica."

"Boy, Jamaica what is wrong with you? I have to work and my bills don't pay themselves," she laughed it off, but I could hear the hesitation in her voice.

"How about this, you come with me and I got you. Don't worry about your bills, your rent none of that shit." I knew that I would beg if she didn't say yes.

"I can't, what about my job? I can't just leave. I have to get approved for vacation time."

"I need you Felicia, I've never needed anybody and right now I need you. I will pay your bills for a year if you say yes, but I need you to spend this time." If she said no it would drive me crazy.

"If you're serious then I'll go, but I don't have a passport."

"Well you have two weeks to get one, I'll call you back to let you know when we're leaving, don't worry about packing cause you can get all new shit," I hung up feeling on top of the world. Finally, I would see her again.

Felicia

I didn't know what type of trouble he was in, but it must be serious if he was offering to pay my bills, let alone for a year. In all of the time I've known him, he has never offered to do anything more than buy my food or take me out. Except for the occasional gift or two. I called my friend Chanel hoping she could give me some much needed advice.

"Yo, Chanel, you won't believe what just happened, Raheim just called asking me to go to Jamaica!" The words rushed from my mouth like running water.

"WHAT! Girl, I know your ass said yes. Right?"

"Yeah, I'm going," I said and she screamed into the receiver making me regret telling her.

"Yo, I knew his ass couldn't stay away from you. You two are made for each other. Well, while you out getting your groove back," she continued, "tell that nigga to put a ring on it!" In spite of how I felt I couldn't help but laugh along with her. Chanel was my closest friend and she always knew what to say to either piss me off or make my day. Today was a good day. I wasn't sure what I needed to do to get my passport, but the Internet was my first move.

Raheim Starz

Amir wanted to meet at Denny's, said he had something important he wanted to discuss. I knew that his definition of important was either bible study or his mom, and the only thing I was willing to hear was how the Lord could save me from this drama. A few heads turned when we walked in. I noticed how a few of the girls threw glances over in our direction. I wasn't fazed about any of it at the moment, not until I knew who had it in for me.

"So what's up?" Amir started off like I'm the one who called this meeting.

"You tell me, give me the short version because I don't have all day," I replied. I hated being rude, but also hated feeling like he was about to set me up.

"I wanted to talk about your-" His sentence was cut off by a cute waitress holding two menus and a smile.

"Sorry to interrupt, but would you like anything to drink to get you started?" Her eyes darted back and forth and I knew she was asking herself who looked better. Amir asked for what he always asked for.

"A glass of ice water please." I ordered orange juice; she sat the menus down, and walked in the direction of the kitchen.

"You know, it's no secret that our mom wants to talk to you." He started the conversation.

"Tell me why I am supposed to care about what she wants again?"

"Raheim you really need to grow up, she is still your mom whether you like it or not and she at least needs to be given a chance," Amir huffed and stared me down again, which always pissed me off when he talked about Janet.

"I'm tired of having this same dumb ass conversation, so let's change the subject before it makes me angry." I felt my blood boiling and I knew I wasn't going to be able to control my temper.

"Cool, but wanted you to know that I'm going up to visit her this Wednesday, and if you're in, you can meet me at the bus station near Frankford."

I no longer felt hungry.

"Listen, because this is the last time you will hear me say it. I don't care about Janet, about visiting her sorry ass in prison and she can stay there until the day her ass dies. She has you psyched up believing she killed him for us. She did that shit for her damn self. She couldn't stand being left behind, thrown away and granted his ass was just as trifling, but she made the decision to open her legs and make babies. She wanted to trap his ass and when that shit ain't work, she went crazy. I see through her bullshit whether you ever choose to or not." I saw the tears building up in the corners of Amir's eyes and I tried not to feel bad. I didn't want to transfer my anger on to him, but he keeps trying to get me to forgive her. As far as I'm concerned, Janet Starz is an illusion, an egg donor who no longer exists. The sooner my brother realizes that the happier we both will be.

Amir's fist clinched and before I could do anything he swung at my face landing a

strong right hand to my eye.

"Yo, what the fuck?" Within moments he was across the table giving me blow after blow. I could no longer see my brother, but a man who deserved to get his ass beat. I jumped up from my seat and drove into the side of his head with a punch so hard my knuckles hurt. His knees buckled and he collapsed on the floor. People were screaming and pushing each other out of the way. The Denny's manager a short, stocky lady with acne scars started shouting for us to leave. I grabbed Amir by his forearm and dragged him to my rental car.

"Get in! Yo get the fuck in before somebody call the police!" I rushed to the driver side and sped off before one of the nosy people standing in the door got the bright idea to call the cops.

"What is wrong with you?" I yelled at him.

"You keep disrespecting my mom and I swear I will hurt you Raheim!" He spoke like a true thug.

"Oh now Mr. Holy wants to fuck somebody up. Let me explain something to your young ass. I'm not pushing Janet down your throat- it's you! I say leave it alone, you still forcing me to swallow it. So how about this, don't talk to me about her ass again. I don't care and probably never will, and if your dumb-ass gets the bright idea to swing on me again, you better make sure you knock me out."

A part of me felt proud of my little brother, this was his first fight and in spite of the blaring pain in the back of my eyelid I thought he did pretty good.

"Why you ain't never tell me you had a mean right hand?" I asked like a proud father.

"Because you never asked," he stared out the window and we rode the rest of the way in silence.

Chapter Five:
Just Getting Started

Everyone in my man's crew sat around my living room table. They were all itching to pay that pretty nigga back.

"Listen, I don't need anyone else to handle this, but me. I want to teach him a lesson that he will never forget." I looked over at Drake, his face was still wired up and he already lost about ten pounds since the incident.

"Yo, while you thinking up a strategy that muthafucka is acting like he invincible," Ray said angrily.

"I want him to get comfortable so I can attack when he least expect it. I got this." Drake started writing on his legal pad. Everybody stopped to watch; whatever Drake said would be how it went down. He flipped the tablet for everyone to see.

Let my baby do it her way, when she needs help

Y'all niggas swoop in and take that nigga out

Everyone nodded in agreement and it was final. They had to give me respect and I was determined to make him pay. I already had him shook and that's exactly where I wanted him. I needed to move at a pace that would allow him to almost forget. So it's cool that he's starting to get comfortable. My next move was already in motion and I couldn't wait to get it started. My girl Pam told me he had a little brother and I already had plans for him. Soon I was gonna have Pam attend his church to get close to his brother making sure she sat close enough for him to take notice.

"Jackie? You sure you got this?" Ray asked more aggressively.

"Yeah I'm sure; y'all need to stop underestimating me. His ass is already shook and I know where he lay his head at night." I didn't want Ray and his crazy ass friends to handle anything because they were all trigger-happy. The last thing I needed was to have a sloppy job land me in prison for murder. I walked everybody to the door so I could take care of my man.

Raheim Starz

I lay in my bed staring up at the ceiling, frustrated that I couldn't sleep. It was Wednesday and despite how much I wanted to forget about Amir going up to the prison I couldn't. Though I try to show the world my tough guy demeanor Janet hurt me. Not because she killed my father, but because she threw me away like I didn't mean shit to her. I felt like a pawn in her wicked game and when things didn't go her way she tossed me to the side with no hesitation. I forced myself to change my thoughts before my attitude changed.

Felicia called earlier to let me know she had already submitted her application for her passport. I was happy as hell that I would be out of the country in a few days. A month of relaxation would be enough time to let things blow over. I still didn't know who the crazy broad in the silver Infinity was but she hasn't struck again so I guess she was happy with busting out my windows.

Not seeing any of my regular girls has put a huge hole in my social life and has my phone blowing up 24/7. I think it's about that time to get a new number anyway. Get a new arsenal of ladies, but this time I would be damn sure to do a pre-screening first. I pulled myself out of bed and took a quick shower. I had some business to take care of with Maya and Alexis before I went off to sunny Jamaica. Janet's letters fell out of the closet when I reached in to get a pair of my Roca Wear jeans. I only read the one letter from Janet, but there were two left unopened. I didn't feel like the drama, so I tossed them both back on the top shelf of my closet. Sure they would be there until I had enough courage to open them or throw them in the trash.

Janet Starz

I haven't seen Amir for a few months and I was extremely excited. He told me he was going to ask Raheim to come today and since I didn't hear anything I assumed he was successful. I shampooed my hair and had Carla braid it into two Indian braids. I tried my best to appear apologetic and vulnerable because I needed Raheim to get sucked into helping me out of this hellhole. My C.O came to the cell to inform me that I had a visitor. I knew she was going to have to handcuff my wrists and ankles before we walked off the block and through the adjacent building into the visiting room. I put my arms out without her asking and for the first time since I've been here, I didn't mind the cold metal touching my skin. A lot of the bitches stopped talking when I walked by, which made me think they were talking about me. I kept looking straight ahead, because today I didn't give a fuck about none of their raggedy asses.

My heartbeat picked up as we got closer to the visiting area. I could see the door that read off the rules

No Touching
No Loud Talking
& No Kissing

I took a few deep breaths and tried to calm down before we reached the door. My C.O went through her usual check.

"Open your mouth, shake your head and remove your shoes." She slid her hands up and down my inner and outer thighs, turned my shoes upside down and shook them before allowing me to put them back on. Once she gave me the go ahead she unlocked the cuffs and opened the visiting door. I saw Amir standing alone and my heart sank. His eyes were saying sorry and then I became angry, but stuffed the emotion down into the pit of my stomach. I didn't want him to feel like I was ungrateful for his visit. In spite of the sign I gave him a quick hug and we sat down at the orange round table.

"I told him I was coming today but he didn't want to hear it," Amir said.

Platinum Dust

"No, no it's cool, I'm happy to see you here," I said, giving him a reassuring smile even though I was pissed. Who the fuck does Raheim think he is? I gave him life and he thinks he can keep giving me his ass to kiss. Amir went on and on about his schoolwork and what he was doing now. He didn't want to answer me when I asked about the light bruise around his temple. Finally he admitted that he had a fight, but didn't want to tell me who with. It didn't take much time for me to guess. I needed to step up my game and play my hand a little better. Pleading for Raheim's sympathy was the wrong approach I needed to take it back to his level. The three-hour visit was over before I could blink and before I knew it, the loudspeaker was announcing visiting hours were coming to an end.

"I will keep trying for you Mom. Raheim is still upset but I think he'll come around," Amir looked me in my face and told me a lie. His brother wasn't going to come around, because he was just like Carlos. He held on to a grudge and did what he wanted to do. I went back to my cell with a long face.

"So, what happened? Did he show up?" Carla was waiting for the juice, but I didn't feel like her and all of her 50 questions. I kicked off my shoes and flopped on my thin mattress, turning my back to face her and tried to go to sleep. I needed a new strategy, because waiting until he came around would be like waiting for hell to freeze over.

A few hours had passed since my visit but I still didn't feel like leaving my cell. I couldn't believe I was this upset about something I already knew might not happen anyway.

I rethought about the letters I sent him and what I could have added that may have changed his mind. I should have told him that I wish I could take it all back. Either way I started feeling the concrete walls closing in around me. I would be here for the rest of my life and it was finally sinking in. My parents didn't have any money and Amir was in school so he couldn't help me with a good lawyer. Two girls that knew Raheim before they were put on lock down let me know that he drove around in an Expedition, wore the freshest gear and didn't mind spending a few dollars when necessary.

"Lights out!" the C.O shouted after our last head count and I was more than glad to be in silence. The constant chatter during the day could be deafening.

The next morning, the sunlight from the common area lit my small cell and metal clanking against metal as the rude ass correctional officers struck the bars with their nightsticks. I jumped out of bed, more from frustration than anything else, waiting for them to do another count. Carla stood beside me wiping the sleep from her eyes. I was so over this bullshit, being told what to do and when all damn day was enough to drive any sane person crazy.

"So I guess he didn't show up huh? Carla asked with a questioning tone.

"No bitch, now what? Whatever you have to say about it hurry up so I can get on with my day!" I snapped, turning to look her in the eye as I spoke.

"Damn Janet, nobody gone bust your balls for wanting to see your son. Calm your ass down. I'm just asking cause

I know how excited you were, whether your ass want to admit or not." She was right, a part of me wanted to see Raheim. I haven't seen him since he was 11 years old, but I need to stop fucking dreaming and come back to the real world."

"It'll be time for breakfast in a minute so you better brush your teeth," I changed the subject and lie back on my bed. I didn't feel like eating another dry ass breakfast of cereal, a banana and a glass of orange juice.

I skipped breakfast because I needed to work on a new strategy, something completely different from what I've been doing. Right when I was ready to set pencil to paper my C.O came to let me know I had a visitor.

"I'm not expecting anybody," I told her.

"Well, I'm not your damn messenger, you have ten minutes to get yourself together," she walked away with her keys smacking loudly against her hips. It could only be one thing, bad news. No one ever visits without telling me first especially on a weekday. I only hoped nothing happened to my mom, she looked pretty sick the last time she was here. She tried to fake it like everything was fine. But she looked old and had a head full of salt and pepper hair. I wouldn't be able to take it if something happened to her while I was in here.

I quickly dressed and washed my face again. I didn't care that my hair was a bit messed up from sleeping on it and my eyes were a bit puffy. My C.O came back and placed the cuffs back around my wrists and ankles, only this time, I hated the hard metal pressing into my flesh. I walked the same corridor from yesterday, only today, I felt like it was leading me to my own funeral. I dreaded seeing my father or aunt there to tell me my mother had passed away. Every scenario that could play in my head did and I reread the same set of rules while my C.O unlocked my wrists and told me to, "Open your mouth, shake your head and remove your shoes." I did all three with my heart beating fast and hard. Finally she opened the visiting room doors and I hesitated a moment before walking through.

My eyes scanned the room before resting on a tall figure with their back toward me. I didn't recognize this person and figured they must have the wrong inmate. Just when I turned to look at the guard's booth the man turned around, causing my breath to catch in my throat.

"Carlos?" I whispered quietly, my eyes squinted in disbelief. He didn't move only stared at me with his beautiful green eyes. I walked over to him like a lamb being led to the slaughter.

"Raheim?" I asked barely above a whisper before I dropped in the chair in front of the orange round visiting table. My legs couldn't support my body; he stood over me for a brief moment before sitting in front of me. My heart raced and my head started pounding.

We both stared at each other in silence for five minutes. I couldn't believe how much he looked like Carlos, how manly he looked. Everything I planned on saying flew out of the window and a lump took its place in my throat. Before I could prevent myself, my eyes began to water and the tears flowed like a river. I put my face in my hands and cried for every sin I ever committed. Through blurred tears I watched a range of emotions cross Raheim's face. He went from confusion, anger, disbelief and finally grief as he watched me cry. I tried to compose myself before the guards came to cut our meeting short.

"I wasn't expecting you to come." I said barely above a whisper.

"I didn't plan on coming here either, but I have some questions that I need to have answered." I knew this would happen and I just prayed I would have the right answers he needed especially since my whole life depended on it.

"Ok."

"Why did you do it?" His voice cracked and for a moment I thought he would break down, but he didn't.

"My letters explained why-" he cut me off before I could get to the end of my explanation.

"Fuck your letters, I want to know how can you kick your kid out of the house and never look back?" The look of anger and pain spread across his face.

I really didn't have an explanation, but I would have to give him one.

"I was hurting at the time and I couldn't think clearly Raheim. I swear I wish I could take it back because I would."

"You know what is real fucked up? Your ass didn't think about nobody but yourself. You said to hell with being a mom and killed a nigga you already knew was no good. You fucking left me and Amir like you was on some ole' hero shit, like we supposed to be proud of your ass or something." His words were pure venom, lethal and deadly.

I was speechless and his words stung, but I took it. He had a right to vent and I would give him that much.

"Do you know what it's like to have what you've always wanted placed before you then to have it snatched from you within a moment's notice? Do you know what it's like to look two little kids in the face who didn't deserve the life you created for them? Before you go off judging me you may want to live in my shoes." His face twisted into a look of disbelief.

"Live in your shoes huh? Well are those the same damn shoes that walked me to my aunt's house seven hours away? Or how about the same shoes that left you mother and fatherless, tell me something Janet did you really want kids or did you think we would help you hold onto your man?"

As much as I wanted to give him a chance to express himself, I couldn't tolerate the disrespect.

"Wait a minute Raheim, You don't have to like me, but you will at least talk to me like you got some damn sense. I loved your father more than the air I breathed and I couldn't have him thinking it was ok to treat me or my kids like we ain't mean shit." My voice elevated with each word.

"Do you know how fucking low you made me feel? I don't give a damn about Carlos or what the fuck he did to you, but I didn't do shit and had to pay for it. You know what? I'm out; I should have never come here in the first place." He moved his chair back like he was ready to leave.

My heart beat quickened knowing that this was my only chance to change his mind.

"Wait! Listen, I know what I did was wrong but I made you leave to protect you!" At that moment I stopped caring about the nosy broads sitting in the chair a few tables over. Many of them were ear hustling and a few were staring lustfully at my oldest son. I didn't have time to gloat or even feel good. I needed him to pick up what I was putting down.

"Protect me from who?"

"ME!" I shouted. One of the C.O's tapped his nightstick against the table, indicating I was breaking one of the rules. For a moment there was silence and I never felt more like hiding under a rock than in this moment. His green eyes studied my face like he was making a mental picture. This was it and I knew he would never come back. He had his answers, whether he wanted to hear them or not. Now I would be left with all of the hurt to dwell on for the rest of my life. He took a deep breath and stood up. An officer came over to the table and he let him know he wanted to leave.

I felt rage building up inside of me and before I knew it I was screaming at him.

"You selfish bastard, why the fuck would you come here to torture me?" Two correctional officers rushed over grabbing me by the arms.

"Why the fuck did you come? YOU act just like your FATHER." I felt my feet kicked from under me and my face hit the cold, hard linoleum floors as they cuffed me.

"Wait, Your HURTING ME!" I shouted to the officer with his knee in my back.

"Calm down Ms. Starz," someone said. Another C.O. made the other inmates line up against the wall with their hands on their heads in the midst of my commotion. Raheim turned to look at me, shaking his head, before he was escorted out of the building and it was just like watching Carlos' smug ass laugh at me all over again.

Raheim Starz

I used to think people who said they needed closure were a bunch of sucka's. But after leaving Janet's crazy ass back in the visiting room, I realized it was important. I needed to ask her that question face to face, so I could see her answer. I almost felt sorry for her- until I saw her acting all crazy. I didn't mean shit to her and I needed to come to grips with that. I didn't tell Amir I was coming because I wanted to talk to her on my own. I didn't need him there when I said what I had to say. When I reached my rental in the prison parking lot I sat behind the wheel for a few minutes thinking. Unexpected tears welled in my eyes and I cried for the first time since I was a kid. I didn't give a damn who was watching me. I thought seeing Janet would be different or that she would hug me and apologize.

"Cut the weak shit Raheim," I shook myself, wiping my eyes with the back of my shirtsleeve. It's time to walk away and never look back. I turned the radio on and blasted the volume; I didn't want to think about Janet, Amir, Carlos and I damn sure didn't want to think about the kid I used to be. I felt my cell vibrating in my pants pocket, reminding me to turn it back on. Felicia's name popped up on the screen making me smile. I turned the volume down before answering.

"Rah?"

"Hey girl, what's up?" I forced myself to sound happy as I headed out of the prison parking lot onto a tree-lined road.

"My passport came today. I had it expedited 'cause I didn't know when you wanted to leave."

"Good, cause I swear I'm tired of Philly. Let's leave tomorrow!" I could hear the excitement in her voice when she yelled, "OK!"

I was going to Jamaica and I could leave all of my drama back in the city streets of Philadelphia. I went back to my apartment to get a carry on bag. I told Felicia to pack light, only enough clothes for one bag to eliminate suspicion. Two black people going out of town with no luggage didn't look right to me. I already notified Maya and Alexis that I would be away for a while. I trusted them, but knew anything could go wrong at any minute. All of my connections paid me directly and I wired funds into both girls' accounts. There wouldn't be any problems on my end. I made sure of that and I had enough info on each of my corporate connections to guarantee loyalty. I would have to drop off a few stacks to my aunt Sadie to keep her covered for a few weeks. After my uncle died I knew she wouldn't be able to survive on those little ass social security checks.

Amir wasn't talking to me and I really didn't care, but I loved my brother so I sent him a text letting him know he could call me if he needed anything. I couldn't wait to get on the plane to Jamaica with my girl Felicia. I swear I planned on forgetting where I came from the minute my foot hit the island. On my way to my aunt's I decided to do a quick stop over my man Dre's crib on Woodland Ave. The streets looked dirtier every time I drove through. Before I could knock on the door it swung open. Dre's face softened from a death stare.

"Yo hurry up and step inside!" I looked over my shoulder when I noticed his hand touching the butt of his gun.

"What's up? Why you so paranoid?" I asked, as Candy appeared in the doorway wearing more clothes than I've ever seen her in.

"Dre got some bad news yesterday and now he thinks everybody out to get him," she smirked and walked back into the kitchen.

His two front men stood watch by the door and the windows.

"My boy Tony told me that he heard about your Expedition from a chick who knows his girl."

My heart started racing, finally I would have a clue.

"And?"

"His girl said you may want to watch your ass. Somebody got a hit out on you and this time they coming hard."

"Yo, what the fuck is happening? I swear this is some real twilight zone shit. I don't know who got beef or what the hell this shit is about but it don't matter I'm out tomorrow morning." For a moment I saw Dre's face change. I knew he thought I was a coward, but I didn't give a damn, I'm not built for all this thug shit.

"Yo man I need you to be safe and call me when you get to where you're going." We did our usual handshake before I rolled out. This time I watched the streets more carefully; everyone was a potential suspect including the innocent looking old lady crossing the street. I bobbed in and out of traffic taking the long route to my aunt's house. The door was unlocked like usual but this time my aunt was upstairs in her bedroom. I knocked twice before she answered.

"Amir?"

"No it's Raheim, listen I'm going out of town for a few weeks, so I wanted to stop by with a few dollars." She opened her bedroom door with her hair in rollers.

"Where you going?" the only time she put rollers in her hair was when she planned on going out with Ms. Val.

"My man died two years ago!" she remarked before walking back over to her vanity. I slid a thick envelope between her jewelry box and her makeup bag.

"Me and Val are going out since you need to be in my business. Where are you going, is the question!" She stopped for a moment to look at my reflection in her mirror.

"I'm taking Felicia to Jamaica; I need to get away for a bit, clear my head you know?"

"Who is Felicia? She must be something else anytime your ass is paying for a trip," she smirked and for a moment I saw her freeze.

"What happened?" I asked hesitantly.

"Nothing you looked like your father for a minute. I'm sorry, well you enjoy yourself and be careful." For the first time I realized that Janet took something from my aunt Sadie and that was her brother. That made me angrier, but life goes on right?

I kissed my aunt on her forehead.

"I love you and soon as I get to Jamaica you'll be the first person I dial."

"Listen, Raheim before you go I want you to know that I couldn't have asked God for a better son than you, I love you, even though you ain't taking me to Jamaica," she tried to lighten the mood with a joke.

"Don't worry when I come back we can go anywhere you want," I said. She giggled and swatted me out of her room. I loved making Sadie smile, because she damn sure deserved it.

Felicia

Raheim insisted we sleep in a hotel close to the airport and I was too excited to argue. I slept through the four-hour flight because I knew that taking pills was out of the question. I hated airplanes and the sick feeling I felt in the pit of my stomach during takeoff almost had me ready to confess. The plane landed at the Sangster International airport in Montego Bay and I swallowed hard as nausea tried to consume me. Rah looked sexy as hell in a pair of blue jeans, an off white Giorgio Armani button down and camel colored Ferrini alligator shoes. I pretended we were an actual couple as he put his hand on the small of my back walking off the plane.

"Welcome back to de Island Mr. Starz, gud to see ya gin," A tall, thin older Jamaican wearing plain tan khaki's with a white stripe running down the sides and a white polo shirt reached out his hand to Raheim. "Welcome ma'am" He grabbed for my bag and started escorting us to a classic white van.

"That's Lucius, he's the chauffeur so if you want to go somewhere let him know," Raheim whispered in my ear. I took a moment to take in everything around me. I've never been out of the country and Jamaica was always on the top of my must-do list. Green was everywhere, the tall trees seemed happier here than in the ghettos of Philadelphia. The sky seemed bluer and the birds sang louder. I just knew I was in heaven with a green-eyed angel. I took out my cell phone and started snapping pictures at everything. Chanel and Beverly would be jealous when I called later tonight. When the loud roar of the van's engine started I stopped myself from jerking forward. In one easy movement Raheim lifted his arm around my shoulders and pulled me into him.

"I'm glad I came," I whispered into his chest and he whispered. "I'm glad I asked" into my hair. If people could die from being too happy I was sure my time was soon to be up. Now if I can only manage to hide my pregnancy for the next few weeks we'd be all good. I thought we would be headed to a hotel or resort, but the van kept going down a long, dirt path with tall trees on each side.

"Where we goin?" I looked up at Rah with an undeniable question mark on my face.

"You'll see, sit back and stop asking questions." I liked surprises, but he already surpassed my expectations flying me out in first class, paying my landlord for one year's worth of rent and promising me a new wardrobe. I was officially in heaven, surrounded by beautiful Jamaican people and accompanied by one of the world's finest men. The road ended in front of a tall iron gate surrounded by rose bushes. It opened up to a large private villa. I had to take a deep breath and remind myself that he invited me, not as his woman, but his best girl out of many.

Full figured, brown-skinned Jamaican women, with beautiful white smiles, welcomed me to the Hanover House, a 4 bedroom, 5-bathroom mini Mansion, with large sparkling pool and large water fountains in the front garden.

"Sumting to drink ma'am?" they asked with heavy accents. I froze for a moment I forgot there would be drinks.

"Virgin Strawberry Daiquiri please, I still feel a bit sick from the plane ride," I added for Raheim's sake.

"I'll take a Tallyman," Raheim ordered and led me into the house like he's been here a thousand times. Everything was decorated white and blue in the entryway, with large hanging plants and windows with views of the water.

"I'm glad your ass came, now you can't run or hide," he walked up behind me wrapping his arms around my waist. Squeezing my stomach gently, I tensed for a moment, then relaxed in his arms, praying to God I could conceal my nearly eighteen-week-old secret. So far I was carrying pretty small. Except for the small lump, you almost couldn't tell I was pregnant. I told Chanel and Beverly the news before I got on the plane. They both started yelling and asking what Raheim said when I told him. After five minutes of trying to calm them down, I told them I was letting him know in Jamaica, which was a lie, but I liked how it sounded.

"You need to stop acting like you like me boy," I said and turned to face him, pressing my lips into his and closed my eyes. I haven't had sex since our last encounter and my pussy was jumping. He didn't answer. Instead he lifted me by my waist and I wrapped my legs around his. He walked with me to the master bedroom, kissing and biting my lower lip. I felt my nipples harden and my juices begin to flow. I promised myself not to act so weak when we got here, but that promise flew out of the nearest bay window as he slid his hands under my shirt. My breathing turned into a light pant as he unfastened my bra. I was sandwiched between the wall and Raheim's hard body as his lips pressed against my neck and collarbone.

"Damn girl, I missed you," he whispered.

"Good, now unfasten your jeans." I instructed. I didn't have time for catch up conversations. I wanted to feel him inside of my wetness NOW; we had plenty of time to talk later. I felt him slide his jeans and boxers down over his hips and I knew I was about to be satisfied as his hardness eased inside of me slowly. My body tensed before I pressed down onto his greatness. In one powerful moment, we were both motionless staring into each other's eyes. When the moment passed we were like hungry wolves feeding on our prey. He turned us both around allowing the wall to support his body. I went to work up and down on his magic stick. I loved watching his expression each time I slammed down harder and harder. I heard a light knock on the door before it opened. I immediately felt embarrassed and wanted to stop, but Raheim kissed me.

"I don't give a damn who's here, you're not going anywhere," he said and continued stroking me like a guitar, holding my waist and guiding me up and down on his dick. I tried to ignore the sound of the tray holding our drinks being placed on the table beside the bed. I closed my eyes so I wouldn't see the pretty Jamaican girl watching us shyly as she left the room, locking the door behind her. There was something sexy about not giving a fuck that made me go hardcore. I worked my hips until we both reached our climax. I held onto his neck tightly and he kissed my shoulder as the light breeze from the window cooled our sweat-drenched bodies.

Platinum Dust

Raheim Starz

I couldn't believe how long it had been since I gave it to Felicia. She moved like she missed me and that was fine with me. I'm happy she initiated, because I don't think I could have waited until tonight. We both undressed and I watched her walk naked into the bathroom. She closed the door and seconds later the shower was running. I took this time to call my aunt Sadie. She sounded happy to hear from me and thanked me for the money I left her. She never questioned where I got my money and I never lied about having a career. I never gave her a reason to worry and her only advice was for me to be careful and always watch my back. I guess I shoulda followed those instructions a bit closer. I downed my Talley Man and changed my clothes while waiting for Felicia to come back from the bathroom. Fifteen minutes later, she came out wrapped in a towel and her hair pinned up.

"So, you've been here before?" she asked as I watched drops of water fall from her hair down to the middle of her tits and disappearing under the towel.

"Maybe. Why? You like it?"

"It's aight," she grinned and I couldn't believe I had missed her as much as I did. This whole running for my life bit had me thinking about chillin out. I refused to end up like my dad and I looked too good to end up like Janet.

"You betta drink that before it melts. After you change, we can eat cause I'm starving," I said and left her alone so she could get dressed. If I saw her naked again, I knew we'd never leave the room.

Felicia came down ten minutes later and met me in the kitchen. I told Nina, the chef at Hanover house, to bring our food into the dining room, giving me an opportunity to talk to Felicia for a moment. She didn't ask questions as I led her through the kitchen doors into a long hall and then to the huge dining area filled with fresh flowers.

"Listen. On some real shit, I have to talk to you about a few things," I started. She was the only girl I could tell about my mom and not have it thrown back up in my face. She didn't interrupt me or try to tell me I was wrong and she never once told me I needed to reconcile. What I liked the most was that I dogged Janet's name out, and not once did Felicia try to disrespect her or agree. She just listened and I appreciate her for it.

"Ok," she responded and kissed me before sitting in a wooden wingback chair.

"Amir's been coming at me hard about visiting Janet and a few weeks ago he gave me a few letters that she wrote. I wasn't even gonna read the shit but I did." I took a breath, watching Felicia's face as I talked, "She wrote about why she killed Carlos, but I still see right through her."

"Well, I'm proud of you for even opening up the letters," she said. "I know how you felt about it before."

"Then last week me and Amir got into it and can you believe this little nigga threw a few punches in the Denny's for talking about Janet?"

"Denny's?" She looked amused and for a moment I wanted to tell her she was my baby, but I let it go.

"He told me he wanted us to meet up and then he kept trying to shove Janet down my throat. I told him to stop talking to me about the egg donor and that I don't give a damn what happens to her and his fist clipped my eye." We both started laughing.

"He hit you for real?" she asked in between laughs.

"I had to drag his ass out the Denny's before the manager called the cops! But anyway, he wanted me to go up to see Janet on Wednesday." Her face formed a question mark and I knew what she was gonna ask.

"Did you go?"

"I went yesterday by myself," I confessed. She looked as surprised as Janet was when she recognized me.

"Wow, oh my goodness, wow Raheim. Are you ok?"

"I'm cool, I had to ask her why she left me and shit. All this time, she gassing up Amir's head, but the reality is, she only care about her damn self, you know?"

Though I was trying to play it cool I had to swallow a lump growing in my throat. Felicia walked over to me and sat on my lap. I didn't want to but I buried my face in her chest and cried. She only held me and stroked her fingers in my hair. I hugged her waist tight and never felt so free. She didn't let me go until I took a deep breath. I felt her hands on either side of my face as she looked me dead in my eyes.

"It's not your fault Rah, none of it and if Janet can't love you then she's a bigger fool than I thought she was. I don't know your mom, but I do know you and I swear I wish I could take away some of your hurt, but since I can't, I want you to know I'm here for you and I won't go anywhere unless you want me to." I saw Felicia in a whole new light. It's funny how leaving the country can open your mind. She was one of the finest chicks in Philly, sexy as hell and more intelligent than I gave her credit for and she wanted to talk to me.

"Now where's the food cause I swear I'm hungry," she laughed as she wiped my face with her fingertips. On cue Nina came in wheeling our plates filled with curry chicken, rice and beans, fried plantain and cabbage on a cart.

We spent the rest of dinner cracking jokes and talking about how beautiful she thought Jamaica was. I was happy I was able to experience her first trip. I promised to take her shopping tomorrow. But for now, I thought we should walk over to the beach to watch the sun set.

For the next few weeks I wasn't going to be Raheim the playa, the stressed out fugitive, or even Raheim Starz-son of a dead man and the woman who killed him. I was determined to be Felicia's MAN the whole time I was here. Maybe it was time I started looking to get my shit together, before I lost out on a good thing.

Janet Starz
Two Steps Back

"Ms. Starz, why you have to go and make my job harder?" A young C.O asked as she escorted me through the long corridor to the hole. I was given one week in solitary for disturbing the peace and causing a scene with Raheim. It was like having my own personal flashback. I didn't expect Raheim to look so much like Carlos. It was like looking at a ghost from my past. I knew he would want to know why I kicked him out, but I wasn't prepared for his reactions and seeing him shaking his head at me drove me over the edge. Carlos used to come over, thinking he could fuck me and leave shaking his head when I asked him for money for pampers or food. I hated when he walked away from me, I wanted to shake his ass so he could see that I really loved him. The officer gently pushed me into the small concrete room with no furniture except for a toilet.

"Slide your hands through the bars," she instructed and I followed so she could unlock my cuffs. "You can't go around acting like that, it gets you in trouble."

"Don't tell me what the fuck I can do! I'm grown, GROWN muthafucka! I need to get OUT OF HERE!" I screamed at the tiny officer holding my cuffs and her keys in one hand.

"And how you plan on doing that if you can't even talk to people?" Her words sliced me sharper than any knife. She was right. I couldn't leave if I was acting like a damn fool. I hated being alone in the dark with my thoughts and tonight would be especially hard. I would only have pictures of Raheim flowing in and out of my mind. He brought back memories of being in love and how happy I was to see the baby with his daddy's green eyes.

I had the prettiest baby in the world and I was sure Carlos would be happy to have a son that looked just like him. He came around for a while and filled my head with dreams of being a family. He proudly showed off Raheim to all of his friends and family members. He was a proud dad all the way up until I started telling him I needed him to watch the baby while I went back to school. Then he played the disappearing act, stepping out to see my archenemy Gianni. He knew I hated her ass and he still went after her. I hated not being on top, but I was determined to keep my man. I gave him another son, but by then, it didn't matter- I was sure pussy. The baby mama he knew he could fuck when he wanted to. He came and went when he pleased, finding new project broads to freak. Everybody wanted a piece and soon I was a fading part of history.

I remembered the night I kicked Raheim out like it was yesterday. The night before Carlos called to make sure I would be home so he could stop by. I left my back door unlocked for him like I always did and he slid on through close to midnight. Raheim thought he was old enough to wait up to see his dad, but I wanted him all to myself. Rah's stubborn ass refused to sleep until Carlos came over. Rah gave his dad a hug when he walked in. Carlos looked at me with a relieved expression that I would never forget, like Raheim saved him from something.

"Hey little man, why you still up?" He asked with a smile on his face.

"Cause I wanted to say goodnight," Raheim said happily.

"Well, goodnight. Remember to wake up early on Saturday cause I'm coming to take you and your brotha to see grandma tomorrow." He squeezed him on the shoulder and nudged him in the direction of the stairs. I remembered feeling jealous that he gave him that much attention, but I played it cool cause I just knew he was coming to break me off.

"Baby you know I missed you," I whined in his ear like a bitch and tried to kiss him before I noticed how far he backed up.

"Janet, I came here to tell you that I won't be coming here no more. Unless it's about my kids, please don't call me. I got a new girl and I don't wanna fuck shit up you know?"

"Oh you got a new girl huh? Who the fuck is it Gianni? Who? WHO Carlos? Or is it that bum bitch from 52nd street?" I screamed furiously.

"Don't worry about who she is," he said. When Raheim woke up the next morning acting all happy to see his dad I tried to contain myself. I felt my legs walk into the kitchen ready to pull a knife from the drawer. I felt like hurting him for looking like the bastard who just broke my heart. Raheim didn't know that I had a knife in my hands when I told him to get out. I sent him away to save his life because I knew I was on the brink of crazy and it was no turning back. I hated the idea of him leaving me for someone else. I hated feeling like I was the loser to the finest prize in Philly and I knew then that if he made one slip I would end his sorry life and make him regret the day he fucked me over.

K.C Blaze

Chapter Six:
Jamaican Me Crazy

Six weeks in Jamaica and I felt spoiled. Rah bought me a whole new wardrobe with no limits on brand names. I was told to get what I wanted and don't worry about the price. I tried to tell myself not to get to used to this because it would only be for a minute. Needless to say, I bought a lot of maxi dresses to hide the growing lump. For now we were both cool and for some crazy reason, Raheim had been acting like he wanted to be my man. Last night he took me horseback riding and tonight he wants to go to a pajama party near one of the large resorts. We've eaten in almost every restaurant on the island and gone to numerous clubs. It must be something in the water having a nigga act in love. But whatever it was, I was ok with it. I heard a knock on the bathroom door while I was taking my bath and a second later, the door opened.

"Scuse me ma'am, Mr. Starz ah sey how long yuh ah gon tek?" it was the same pretty girl who walked in the first night me and Rah made love.

"Oh ok, tell him to give me another minute," I replied.

"Ok ma'am I tell him yuh soon come," she said. I wanted to tell her it's a thing called knock and then wait for an answer but I bit my tongue. The party was supposed to start around ten and it was only nine forty-five. So him wanting to rush me meant he really wanted to be there. He bought me a sexy red teddy trimmed in black lace and a pair of red heels. When I stepped into the bedroom he was already there waiting, shirtless and patient.

"When you start rushing me?" I turned my back to him so I could slide the thin red lingerie over my head.

"When you start being shy?" He sounded curious and I had to think fast.

"I can be shy when I wanna be. Only my man can see me naked," I teased but when I turned to see his face he wasn't smiling and I suddenly felt the air shift in the room.

"Oh so you need to hear me say it? Why the fuck you think I brought you here? So we can play house. I been walking round here acting like a nut and your ass act like you didn't get the damn memo," he said looking furious and I didn't know what the hell just happened.

"Wait, what just happened?"

"Felicia, if you don't know what the fuck I'm talking about then, I don't have the energy to explain it," he said and walked out of the room leaving me seriously confused. I wanted to follow after him, but I wasn't that chick and never would be. I figured he would either go to the party without me or sulk like a big baby until I came after him. I took my time doing my makeup, making sure my hair was pulled up in a messy ponytail. I slipped on the red heels and headed out the bedroom down into the large living area. All eyes followed the sway of my hips as I went in search of Raheim. I found him on the wrap around porch.

"What's up with you sexy?" I stood in front of him, staring eye to eye. His green eyes were enticing and the golden brown tint to his skin looked especially perfect under the glow of the Jamaican moon. His hands found their way to my waist and he pulled me into him.

"Your ass is mine, you need to start acting like you know better," he said. For a moment my heart dropped in my chest. He was claiming me, I felt sick all of a sudden.

"Are you saying you're my man?" I tried to play it cool, but I could feel my knees starting to buckle. Thoughts of the baby I was carrying flashed before me and then I felt guilty. Should I tell him or should I leave it alone.

"I'm saying that I think it's time I started chillin. You already know I'm feeling you and at this point I know I don't want anybody else. Is that what you want?" He asked. My words caught in my throat, for as long as I knew Rah I've wanted to hear those words. Shit! His timing couldn't be worse.

"I do want to be yours, but Rah, I think we should talk. I need to tell you something," I took a deep breath, hoping that when I told him I was pregnant he wouldn't release his grip cause I was sure I'd fall.

Before I could form the words, Lucius pulled the van around front and I couldn't be more grateful. "We'll talk later, but for now let's go have fun," he said before taking me by the hand leading me into the van. Fast beating reggae filled the night air the closer we got to the party. Soon I was able to see curvy women walking around in sheer and lace nighties and men wearing boxers, pajama bottoms and some even wore sweatpants. I watched Raheim's chest swell with pride as we walked through the lounge area. I tried to act calm, but I really was seconds away from a panic attack. I tried to focus on the soft blue glow coming from the large outdoor pool.

'Just make it through tonight,' I told myself.

Raheim Starz

I pulled Felicia into the center of the room allowing the rhythm of Elephant Man's "Give Me the Whine" to take over. She went in full gear and started moving her hips in a slow whine speeding up and slowing down again. The party was filled with some of the finest girls on the planet, a few were eyein me hardcore, but I gave Felicia my full attention. Besides, the fastest way to get the pussy is to act like you don't want it. Three songs in and Felicia said her feet were hurtin.

"You can still dance if you want, that chick in black been tryna get your attention all night," she said. I looked over my shoulder at the tall brown girl in the corner. She had hips for days and tits the size of cantaloupes.

"Should I give it to her?" I started dancing in front of Felicia

"Yeah, go give it to her, but not too much. I don't want to have to play anybody up in here tonight." I kissed Felicia before walking over to the lady in black.

"Let's dance," I took her by her hand and watched her smile. She was determined to show me her inner freak on the dance floor as her hips gyrated in time to the Caribbean beat. She turned around wrapping her arms around my neck making sure I felt her body rubbing against mine.

"Is that your wife?" She nodded her head in Felicia's direction.

"My fiancé. Why?" I decided to play along for a moment.

"So that means you're still a free man. Can I see you later?" She asked with no hesitation.

"Damn, you real direct huh?" She inched her face closer to mine still moving her hips to the music.

"I see what I want," She said as she turned her head in Felicia's direction and I knew that she was going to try to kiss me. Before she could, I pulled away.

"No thanks, you're not really my type," I said and walked back over to the table, leaving Miss Jamaica standing alone. The one thing I didn't like was drama, I left Philly to get away from the nonsense and would be damned if I let another chick disrespect my girl.

"I see I have some competition tonight," Felicia started to laugh. "See I told you not to give it to her too good babe. She looked like she wanted to freak you on the dance floor."

"I'm good. I got the finest chick right here so I don't go backwards. You want a drink?"

"Cranberry and Vodka and hold the Vodka." I walked over to the bar to get our drinks when I came back Miss Jamaica was standing behind Felicia whispering in her ear.

"Yo, what you want over here?" I sat the glasses down on the table.

"I just thought your girl should know that you asked to see me later," the words dripped from her full lips like poison.

"Get the fuck outta here; I wouldn't fuck you if somebody paid me. Don't fuck wit me tonight. Either you move your ass or I swear I will move it for you! " Another crazy broad to deal with, she moved to the other side of the table and for a moment I saw how nervous Felicia looked.

"Rah, leave it alone. I know her ass is lying," Felicia stood up and grabbed both drinks. "Come on boo," she said and I followed behind her, happy nobody noticed the commotion.

"Yo, I'm ready to get the fuck outta here," I reached for my phone to call Lucius around with the van and noticed I had six missed calls. My aunt called three times, Kelly my old Tuesday called twice and Dre called me too. I dialed my voicemail straining to hear over the music.

"Raheim, I don't mean to bother you but I haven't heard from your brother in a few days. Just wanted to know if he called you, call me when you get this message." Each of her messages sounded like that so I knew she was worried. Kelly's crazy ass went from screaming into the phone to talking softly.

"Why the fuck you keep ignoring my damn calls Raheim? I need to talk to you. I MISS You boo. Please forgive me. I want to see you tonight so if you interested my back door is unlocked" The last message came from Dre and he sounded a bit paranoid.

"Yo Rah, it's your boy Dre. We need to talk a.s.a.p. hit me up nigga" There was a pause before he disconnected the call. Shit was getting crazy back at home. Lucius pulled around and we got into the van.

"Let me call my aunt real quick." I dialed her number and she answered on the first ring.

"Hello?"

"Yeah Ma, what's going on?"

"Sorry to mess up your vacation, but the last time I heard from your brother he said he met a girl at church. Then he stopped coming over, calling and he don't answer my calls. He never acted like this before so I'm worried about him. You know Amir ain't as street smart as you." She finally took a breath.

"When did he say he met the girl?" I didn't think we needed to worry if he say he met her at church but then again church girls are the freakiest.

"About two weeks ago." She answered.

"Hold up TWO WEEKS ago? So he ain't answer your calls in over two weeks?" My heart started racing. Amir is more responsible than anybody I know.

"No, I thought he answered me once, but he never said anything and the phone went dead."

"Shit! Ok let me get back to you in about an hour."

Felicia leaned forward.

"Is everything ok?"

"Amir is missing and my aunt ain't heard from em in two weeks."

"Oh my God," Felicia said as I dialed Amir's number.

"Hello?" I asked into the receiver after I heard it pick up.

"About fucking time, Amir is a bit tied up right now so you may have to get back to him later," a girl's voice answered making my skin crawl.

"Who the fuck is this? Yo, where is Amir?" I felt my heart starting to race.

"What you thought I was joking? I'm not going to stop until I see blood muthafucka."

"If you touch my brotha I swear I'm gonna find your ass and fuck you up."

"Don't worry the party won't start without ya," the mystery bitch promised. I could hear Amir scream in the background, his voice bouncing around like he was in a cave.

"Get me outta here, PLEASE, please!!!!"

"Ok, ok just tell me who you are and what the fuck have I done to you." I was worried that this crazy bitch was torturing my brother.

"I'm the bitch you shoulda never fucked wit, if you don't know me by now you will when this is all over wit." The line went dead and I swear I felt my heart sink to the bottom of the van.

Felicia read my face and sat forward.

"What? What the fuck is happening?" her voice shook.

"I gotta go back home," I looked Felicia directly in her eyes. "I need you to move faster than this dude. Damn," I yelled at Lucius "I gotta leave tonight."

"I'll pack our stuff," she said.

"No, I need you to stay here. Don't worry about it. I'll be back ok. There's money in the safe on the side of the bed and your plane ticket. If I need you back home, I'll call to let you know." I leaned in to kiss her so she could calm down even though my heart was beating a thousand beats a minute.

"The villa is paid for alright. So you don't have to worry about that," I kept giving her instructions while Lucius drove through the unpaved road.

"Raheim I'm nervous, I don't wanna be here alone," she said. I didn't wanna leave her here by herself but I couldn't have anything happen to her.

"It's only for a week or two. Call up one of your girls and have one of them come up wit you." I had to think fast because before the moon turned to the sun again I had to be in Philly. Some crazy broad had my brotha and this shit just got real serious.

The van parked in front of the door and we both got out jogging through the rooms until we reached the bedroom.

"I'm not packing shit, I just need to go," I turned the dial of the safe to get my plane ticket and jotted the combination to the safe on a post-it beside the bed.

"Yo, keep this in a safe place it's the numbers to the lock. Don't worry I'm gonna come back in a week or so. Ok?" Tears welled in Felicia's eyes causing me to freeze.

She looked scared and I knew its cause she thought she might not see me again.

"Come on babe, don't cry. It's probably nothing. When I come back, I expect you to give it to me like you did the first night we got here," I smiled at her and for a moment she looked ok.

"I gotta go. But I'll call you when I get back ok." I changed my clothes real quick and ran back to the front of the house where I had Lucius run me over to the airport. I didn't know where to look and I needed Dre if I was gonna get a clue. I dialed his number from the back of the van.

"Yo Raheim, what took your ass so long dude?" Dre's deep voice came through on the other end.

"I was wit Felicia, what's good?"

"I found out the chick that put a hit out on you got Amir. I think I know the bitch, but I'm still working on it now."

"I'm on my way back to Philly now. I should be there in a few hours. I called his phone and a broad answered talking about she wasn't gonna stop until she see blood."

"Yo, you need to figure this shit out before Amir's ass is dead. I'll meet you at the airport. I'm gonna let you talk to my man Gutta." We hung up; it felt good knowing Dre still had my back. Amir was like his baby brother too and he liked that he wasn't into the streets. Lucius couldn't get me there fast enough.

Chapter Seven:
Do You Really Wanna Know?

Felicia

Rah wasn't telling me everything. But I knew it was some serious shit going on because he flew outta here faster than a bat outta hell. I felt my stomach tighten and I tried not to panic. My chest heaved in and out until I laid on my back across the king sized bed. Filling my lungs with air and exhaling slowly until my heartbeat went back to normal. This was not how I planned on spending my time in Jamaica, but Amir was in trouble. My mind starting pulling memories of the night Rah came over saying someone tried to kill him. I figured it was a girl with her nose wide open until now. His ass was fine but not fine enough to go to jail for.

For the first time since I've known I was pregnant, I felt a flutter in my stomach. It was so faint I didn't notice it at first but then it happened again. I pressed my hand onto my stomach and felt a small fluttering of movements close to my ribs. It hit home that I was really carrying a baby inside of me and that it was with the one man I wanted most. Instead of making me happy it made me sadder, knowing this baby was going to be another black statistic. I tried not to cry but couldn't help it. Before I knew it, I cried myself to sleep with one hand on my stomach and the other gripping the combination to the safe.

A few hours later and I could feel the sunlight warming the side of my face. A glass of orange juice, two slices of toast and an omelet was sitting on a tray at the foot of the bed. I used the phone on the side of the bed to dial the kitchen.

"Sorry to bother you but can I get a cup full of ice chips please?" I've been having a craving for ice chips for weeks now and don't know what that's all about. I dived into my food feeling extremely hungry and avoided looking on Raheim's side of the bed. For the last few weeks I woke up to him in the morning. Before I could say "come in" my bedroom door was opened by Nellie, one of the housekeepers.

"Mum, see you be wantin a lickle more just call me," she sat the cup of ice on my tray and turned to leave.

"Wait, can I ask you something? Is there any Dr.'s around here?" I didn't want her in my business cause I knew all the tongues in the house would be set ablaze.

"Dr.? Chile you be needin to see Cecily down dere by da market. You feelin sick?" her question was designed for a lesser mind to start talking- but not me.

"A little, but I think it's all this fresh air. Thanks for the ice," I ended the conversation before she could start prying any further. I was about due to see a Dr. I was already at the end of my second trimester and though I felt fine, you never know. After breakfast, I would have Lucius drive me to the market to see this Cecily.

I took a quick shower and put on a colorful ankle length maxi dress that made my breasts look bigger. I took a few hundred from the safe before slipping on a pair of blue flip flops and paging Lucius to meet me at the front of the house. He asked me where to before closing the van doors.

"Cecily down by the market please." He nodded like he knew exactly where to go and we pulled off. I knew this might be the last time I got to see Jamaica, so I paid close attention to everything around me. The tall trees seemed to be leaning forward to offer me shade and the birds seemed to be singing me my own song. The road went from being unpaved and bumpy to being smooth and level. The van stopped just short of an old beat up building. It was two stories high and had a weathered wooden door. Out in front was an old woman with shiny, dark leathery skin. Fine lines were found around her eyes and nose. Her hair shot out from her scalp like a cloud of black and silver smoke forming an Afro. She didn't speak a word, only held out her hand for me to help her stand up. The cool of her palm surprised me in the morning heat. Lucius went back into the van to wait for me. I was a bit freaked out, but waited to see if any shady shit jumped off. She turned to face me before talking.

"So you be lookin for a docta?"

"Yes, I haven't been feeling good." I tried to lie but she cut me off by placing her hands on my stomach. I moved back bumping into a table, I don't know if I was more surprised that she touched me or that she knew what I was there for.

"You about five months?"

"No six and I've only been to see my doctor two times since I've found out."

"Is the baby in dere movin round?" Her expression told me she was about her business, so I decided to answer her questions.

"Yes."

"You from the U.S, I know because yous a skinny lickle ting." She started pulling small jars filled with liquid off of shelves. I hoped she didn't think I would be drinking any of it.

"When you and your husbin going back to the states Chile?"

"I'm not married and my child's father had to go back yesterday for business." For a brief moment I saw a look of judgment cross her aged face and it made tears well in my eyes. I hated being this emotional and it started to feel like everything could make me cry. She wrapped her arms around me and let me cry into her shoulder.

"No worries chil, you'll be fine. Lovin a man is a woman's first curse; her second tis not lovin herself enuf."

Raheim Starz

Dre and his boy Gutta met me at the airport. Dre's whip was a classic Grand Marquis that looked like an old police patrol car, tinted windows and sitting on 22's. We hopped in and Dre sped off in the direction of West Philly.

"Gutta, this my man Rah and he need to hear what the fuck you told me the other day." Gutta turned in the passenger seat to face me. There was nervous energy buzzing in the car and I felt it.

"You pissed off one of the most sadistic bitches out there homie," Gutta started.

"Tell me something I don't know," I said as I worked to control the frustration threatening to creep onto my face.

"My girl is cool wit a chick name Pamela who was sent to get your brother for Jackie-"

"Who the fuck is Jackie dude?" The only Jackie I knew was a girl I messed wit back in high school and I was pretty sure she was married with children by now.

"Jackie mess wit a dude name Showboat," he answered. I saw how tense Dre's shoulders got at the mention of Showboat, but couldn't figure out what this had to do with me.

"No disrespect, but who the fuck is Showboat?" I leaned forward giving Gutta all of my attention.

This time Dre spoke, his voice low and strained like I said something wrong.

"Showboat has been trying to take over my muthafuckin territory for a while now." I could feel my anger rise. Amir was in trouble over territory.

"So what Jackie sayin, I fucked her or some shit?" My question dripped with sarcasm.

"No muthafucka, you broke her man's jaw a while back and now her ass is out to get you for putting him down." The blood rushed from my face causing me to fall back into my seat. Showboat was the dude at club Six-Nine the night I met up with Felicia and her girls. Before I had time to react panic gripped my chest causing me to sweat. I needed air and reached for my window switch. The fresh night air poured into the car quickly cooling my skin.

"I have to get Amir." I said with panic heard in each word.

"I know, don't worry I have a few dudes working on Showboat's location right now. For now, try calling Amir's cell again." I obeyed Dre's request and pulled out my phone dialing Amir's number with lightning speed.

"Hello?" I asked into the receiver. For a moment there was only silence and then I could hear something being ripped and then Amir's voice rush into the phone.

"Raheim? Please help me." He sounded desperate and that made me nervous.

"Amir, listen to me where are you?" I needed him to give me a clue.

"You'll find his ass soon enough," The same voice from earlier came on the line.

"Hey Jackie, won't you stop playing girl. Why the fuck you with a busted ass dude when you can be wit a real dude like me?" I tried to switch up the game. She was a girl and if she mad about her man being put down it had to be about money. I had plenty of that.

108

"What?" I could hear the hesitation and that's all I needed.

"Any man willing to let his woman be in the line of danger is a nut ass dude. If you need money tell me how much and I'll make it happen. Just let my brother go and you can have whatever you want." I put on my best voice praying to God that she would bite the bait and take the offer. For a long moment she didn't say anything and I thought she might take my offer.

"Bitch, I don't want your damn money. I told you what I want and until I get it you won't see his ass again." I heard dead air and knew that I just lost the battle. Dre pulled over and jumped out of the car.

"Yo get the fuck out!" He shouted like he was calling me out.

"What?" I asked confused.

"I said get the fuck outta the car!" He opened the back door and dragged me by my shirt out of the car. I never saw him look so angry at me before.

"Listen, this shit is no joke. You can't keep thinking your ass is gonna pay ya way outta shit. You really don't know who you messing wit son, but you betta wake up real quick. This bitch got your brotha and her ass ain't playin." Seeing Dre so nervous made me worry about Amir more.

"Yo, you betta pray she don't tell Showboat what the fuck you just said or Amir's ass is as good as dead." Gutta added his two cents from the passenger seat. I felt sick and managed to crawl back into the car before my legs gave out. I sat in silence while Dre drove over to another of his cribs in West Philly. My mind kept going back and forth from Amir, Janet and Felicia. The pressure in my head built up until I felt like jumping out of the backseat onto the street. I wouldn't be able to forgive myself if something happened to my baby brother. I waited until we reached the house before I found a room in the back of the house that was unoccupied. I locked the door and dropped to my knees, the weight of my situation weighing heavy on my shoulders. Amir was probably being tortured by a crazy broad who wished he was me. I sent up a prayer to God for him to please spare my brother.

I wasn't sure when I fell asleep but a loud banging on the door made me wake up with a pounding headache.

"Yo Rah, wake up man I need to talk to you," Dre's voice spoke through the door. I scrambled to my feet and unlocked the door to the room.

"We bout to ride out, your ass been sleep for a minute. Showboat's turf is in North Philly so we going to get some answers. I figure his ass know I'm his enemy so he may show his face if he see me around his neighborhood."

"Dre I think we need a better plan. Maybe we been going about this shit the wrong way. We know she has Amir, at this point I need to figure out how to get her to tell me where she at."

"I'm listening."

We already know she don't want money, so the only thing I know for sure she want is my blood. Let's give it to her."

Dre's eyes looked at me with understanding. I would have to get her to trade off. Me for my brother; ain't no point in making him pay for my shit.

"Just give me a minute to think shit through and you get your boys together. Tell em to bring the big guns." Dre nodded before he left me in the room to think about what I just said. I really didn't have a plan but I knew I would need to come up with one.

Within an hour I was standing around a table with some of Philly's hardest bad asses. Trench, known for his ability to shoot a nigga without him seeing it coming, Big Mike, one of the huskiest dudes this side of the Walt Whitman and Crazy Lou, a trigger happy Puerto Rican always itching for a reason to pop one off to name a few. I never thought I would find myself in any of their company but it was what it was.

Dre filled everybody in and a few of them were riled up just from hearing Showboat's name. Dre let them know that we would need their help during the exchange. My job was simply to call Amir's phone to negotiate the trade. If Jackie agreed we would meet them there and ambush when the opportunity presented itself. I knew this wasn't going to be easy but it was a risk I had to take for my brother. When I called his phone no one answered for a few rings and then I heard her voice.

"Jackie?"

"Stop acting like you know me," she sounded frustrated.

"Listen I'm ready to give you what you're asking for. I want to trade me for my brother," The room was so silent you could hear a pin drop. My heart started to pound in the seconds of silence as I waited for her answer.

"I'm so glad you said that big boy, now we play the game. Wait by your phone for my call. I will give you a location and if it looks like your ass has company, I will fucking shoot your brother in his balls." The phone went silent and I felt a mix of relief and dread. I felt a sudden urge to call Felicia; I needed to hear her voice before shit hit the fan. She answered for the first time since I've known her on the first ring.

"Rah?"

"Hey baby, are you ok?"

"No, I felt weird waking up without you this morning. Did you find Amir?" Her question revealed her concern.

"Uh, we're still working on it. Listen I have something I want to tell you," I stood up and walked back upstairs. I wasn't the only one calling their girl. I guess everybody felt the weight of what was about to happen. I waited until the door to the back room was locked before I started talking again. The air felt heavy and my chest felt tight.

"Do you remember the ugly dude from the club I got into a fight wit?

"Uh, yeah. I remember...why?" I could hear her hesitation and it made what I was about to say harder.

"Well his girl kidnapped Amir; she's holding him hostage until she has me."

"Wait, what? Until she has you how Raheim?"

"Listen, I need to say something to you and I need for you to listen to me?" A lump grew in my chest at the thought of what I was about to say.

"I have to get my brother before her crazy ass kills him ok? I need you to know that I love you Felicia. I loved your ass the first time I saw you and I swear I wish I would have told you sooner. If something happens to me-" She interrupted me.

"Raheim, what are you talking about?" She screamed into the phone and I knew she was crying from how her voice was shaking. I felt the energy leave from my arms and legs. "No, wait Raheim, listen I need to tell you something-" A beep came through on my other end and Amir's number flashed across the screen.

"Shit, Felicia I gotta go, if you don't hear from me by tomorrow get on a plane. I love you!" I clicked over with Felicia's voice screaming my name in the background.

I couldn't allow the heart wrenching sound of Felicia's voice to distract me as I clicked over. I needed to focus on getting my brother before this chick really went crazy and did something I'd catch a case over.

"Meet me at the old warehouse off of 291 over by the airport at 8 tonight. If you bring anybody with you, I swear I will kill you and your punk ass brother!" She almost sounded like she was getting enjoyment out of this.

"How do I know you won't do that anyway?"

"You don't, but it looks like you have no other choice now. Do you?" she hung up with the sound of her laughter ringing in my ears. I ran down the stairs into the living room of Dre's house like a mad man. Dre picked up on my agitation and jumped out of the chair he was sitting in.

"It's on, they want me to meet them at the old warehouse building over by the airport at 8'oclock. We have to do this right cause my baby brother's life is on the line." I put on my brave face, but I had never been in any situation even close to this level of intensity before. I was half scared, half anxious, and part I don't give a fuck.

Dre took over where I left off with a pep talk of his own.

"We have a few hours before we need to roll out. I can't promise any of you niggas you'll be coming home tonight. So if you want to walk, now is the time to do it. But if you wit it, meet back here at six. If you've got a wife or a girl you may want to pay her a visit if you know what I mean."

Thoughts of Felicia lying next to me in bed made me wish she were here now. It just became real and I knew I would have to visit my aunt's house before we left for the warehouse. I needed to make sure she knew about Felicia. Planned or unplanned she had my heart and I had to take care of her if I didn't make it out of this shit tonight.

Felicia

My heart jumped out of my chest when Raheim told me someone kidnapped Amir. I knew he wouldn't stop until he had his brother. Even if it meant he was killed in the process. I had to get home and now! I couldn't pack fast enough. I would only take what could fit in my carryon bag, everything else was unnecessary. I turned the dial of the lock on the safe and put ten one hundred dollar bills in my purse, along with my airplane ticket. On my way to the shower my stomach began to cramp, dropping me to my knees.

"What the-?" I asked no one in particular as I rubbed my stomach in a circular motion hoping the pain wasn't anything serious. The last thing I needed was to have my baby prematurely in Jamaica. Calm down Felicia, you will be ok, just make it home to your man, I told myself. I inhaled and exhaled in deep breaths trying to calm myself down and I felt the baby moving around some more.

"We need to get home before we lose your daddy. Please work with me here," that was the first time I spoke directly to the baby growing inside of me and I swore the cramps stopped and I moved as fast as I could into the shower. Within thirty minutes, I was washed and changed and making my way to the front of the house for Lucius to transport me to the airport. An unfamiliar number flashed across my phone.

"Hello?"

"Felicia?" a woman's voice asked hesitantly.

"Yes, who's this?" This was all becoming scarier by the minute. I didn't know if I could take anything else today.

"It's Raheim's aunt Sadie. Listen honey, Raheim was just here and asked that I pick you up from the airport tomorrow. He doesn't want you to go home until he knows it's safe."

"I'm on my way to the airport now." Before I could control myself, I started to cry into the phone like I knew his aunt all of my life. He talked about her enough for me to feel like I did.

"Is he ok? Did he tell you where he was going? I have to see him," I gasped for breath.

"No honey, but we can talk when you get here ok? Call me when your plane lands ok?"

I would die of guilt if I didn't tell Raheim that I was pregnant before the sun set tonight. He had to know and I owed it to him to tell him before he went out risking his life behind a no good muthafucka starting shit at a club.

'Please get me to the airport as fast as you can," I slammed the van door and listened as the old truck's engine roared to life. We began to speed down the winding road in the direction of the airport. Jamaica was the sweetest, most exhilarating vacation I have taken in my life and I would always remember this is where I became Raheim Starz' woman.

"God please let him live or let me die with him," I sent up a silent prayer at the same moment my baby kicked me in the ribs.

Chapter Eight:
My Brother's Drama

Amir

The dim light in the small room I was kept in flickered on and off, making me feel on edge. My hands were tied tightly behind my back cutting into my already raw skin. My nose stung with the stench of my own sweat and the dank musky scent that oozed from the walls. I knew I was in a warehouse but didn't know where. Footsteps echoed and bounced around the building and I could hear the angry, sadistic shouts every time my kidnapper talked to my brother. I just kept praying to God to forgive me for my moment of weakness that led me to my present dilemma It wasn't until I was hit over my head that I realized I was a pawn in Raheim's drama. I lost track of the days and only knew that I had to get out of here alive.

These chicks were crazy as hell itself and visited me throughout the day to help me to the bathroom or to feed me fast food burgers, which I normally despised but ate out of starvation. Occasionally Pam, if that was her real name, came in to screw me without my consent. But I was tied and the flesh is weak. Betrayed as well by my lower half, always willing to rise to the occasion. I kept going over my last week of freedom and cursing myself for falling into this obvious trap. I should have known she was way too good to be true.

I hadn't seen her in church before and she sat a row in front of me during church service. I tried not to stare at her but she was beautiful. Her skin was the color of cinnamon and she had the perfect silhouette. I wasn't usually weak when it came to women, primarily because I really did want to wait until marriage and all that good stuff. Unlike my brother I still believe in love, and I learned from what my parents did to each other. I wanted the type of love my aunt Sadie had with my uncle, but I also believed in forgiveness and my mom needed tons of it. That is why Pam was so appealing. She seemed innocent and God-fearing. She wasn't all eager to jump up in my face like most of the other girls in the church. She didn't flirt with me and that caught my attention. After each church service, members usually walked around greeting newcomers and I thought I'd say a quick hello. She was warm and receptive and even smiled, though I saw her eyes light up just a little when she first saw me, she didn't come on to me. I was extremely surprised when I saw her again at Wednesday night bible study and she even sat directly across from me so I could see her pretty face. I tried to remain focused during the pastor's message but it was hard. By Friday night's prayer meeting I was running in to see if she was there and she was. Only this time she asked to share my bible because she forgot hers at home and we prayed holding hands until the prayer meeting was over.

I struck up a conversation after the meeting and she answered all of my questions until we were both laughing and sharing stuff about our lives. I didn't realize that all of that sharing was to get information on Raheim. We were inseparable for two weeks calling each other every day and night and seeing each other before, during and after the prayer meetings, bible studies and Sunday church services. My weakest moment came when I kissed her out of nowhere after walking her to her car and I swear that was the best kiss I ever had.

I couldn't stop thinking about her and gladly accepted her offer to come to a 'bible study' at her house. She told me to meet her on 69th street by the tower theatre at 8:30pm. When I got there, a black Ford Explorer with tinted windows pulled up in front of me. The window rolled down just enough for me to see her and then the doors opened up with two big dudes jumping out to hustle me into the SUV. One held my arms while the other put a cloth up to my nose. I can't remember much after that except waking up in this ridiculous room in my boxers and handcuffed. I was still confused until a short brown skinned woman came in talking at me before hitting me over the head with a hard metal object. Screaming about it being Raheim's fault. Right when the crazy woman was about to hit me in the head again Pam came outta nowhere screaming for her not to hurt my face. She wouldn't look me in the eyes for the first few days.

However, her guilt didn't keep her away for too long cause a few days later she came in apologizing for everything and that she was forced to do it while she rode me into repentance. Periodically the other chick would come in saying it was a shame I was so fine but she had to do what she had to do. Which also meant she had to beat me for the sins of my brother. I refused to cry out when she hit me and that made her angrier. A few times I told her I would pray for her and I hoped God could forgive her in spite of her sins. That usually got her to stop and to walk out of the room.

I could hear footsteps getting closer to my holding room. I knew they were Pam's. Being here left me with nothing better to do but memorize sounds. The door cracked open and she slipped inside of the room. Even in the dim light I could tell she was worried about something.

"Listen, this is starting to get outta hand. I know you probably hate me but I swear I didn't want things to go this far."

"What are you talking about? What's happening?" I asked confused.

"Be quiet, I'm not supposed to say anything. I will come back later but I swear I'm sorry," she said as she walked up to my chair and kissed me on my lips like she didn't expect to see me later. That scared me and caused my heart to start beating outta my chest. What was about to happen?

"Pam, please tell me, is something wrong with my brother?" tears welled up in my eyes. I needed to get out of here and the only way I knew how was to fight my way out, but my hands were tied.

"Your brother is coming at 8, he's gonna trade places with you. I promise I will come back in an hour, just give me some time."

After what felt like hours in silence, I could hear voices bouncing all over the walls. Some of the voices were deeper than what I was used to. They were men, some laughing while others shouted orders. I strained to hear what they were talking about. Though my arms were tied, I could still stand and walk closer to the door. One of the deeper male voices was saying that he won't know what hit him, and let's see how pretty his ass is when I finish with him. I assumed the "he" they were talking about was Raheim, but I couldn't understand why he was in so much trouble. I knew one day his weakness for multiple women would eventually catch up with him, but this was a bit more dramatic, even for him. I walked quickly over to my chair when I heard Pam's footsteps coming closer to the door again.

"I'm gonna loosen your handcuffs but please don't try to get out until I give you a signal." She walked behind me and loosened the grip on the handcuffs. My skin was raw and irritated but felt instant relief from the metal baring into my skin.

"In another life we coulda been together," she said.

"We can still be together. I know this isn't you. I've seen the real you Pam and I swear I won't be mad if you help me get outta this situation. I'm not sure what my brother did, but if I can just talk to him we can probably find a solution." I tried to reason with her.

"Amir, they not tryna hear your gospel, bible toting solutions. Your brotha broke Showboat's jaw in three different places and he crushed his windpipe. What makes it worse is that his boy Dre is Showboat's enemy. They out to get revenge and it ain't nothing nobody can do about it." She shook her head like she thought I was crazy or naïve I couldn't tell.

"God can do something about it," I tried to convince myself of that.

"Then you betta start praying now then." She kissed me again and walked out of the room. Sweat beads started forming around my eyebrows. I was getting more nervous and more agitated. I figured out that my hands could actually squeeze out of the handcuffs with a little prying. I was determined not to die like this. I refused to let my brother die like my father, over a woman. A calmness washed over me and, for the first time since I arrived here, I felt at peace. However, a sinking feeling let me know that I would need more than just prayer if I wanted to make it out of here alive. When Pam left I could hear a dude shout.

"Yo, why you keep going in that room?"

"Mike go ahead wit all dat," Pam yelled back but the dude kept going. His voice sounded like it was getting closer.

"I'm not fucking joking Pam. Why the fuck you keep going in there? Don't tell me you caught feelings for that muthafucka!" Before I knew it I could hear Pam scream and the room door flew open. Pam looked weak in comparison to the tall muscular dude gripping her by the arm. He had a huge pistol in his hand and he pointed it right at my chest.

"Now tell me again, did you catch feelings for this nigga?" He sounded like the wrong answer would most definitely result in my death. She stared me directly in the eyes and shouted.

"Hell NO! Now stop tripping and get off my damn arm, you're hurtin me." She yanked her arm away and turned out of the room. I knew she just saved my life and I knew she was lying but I didn't have time to think about that right now. Before he turned to leave he walked up to within an inch of my face and punched me in my stomach hard enough to make me hurl yesterday's lunch. I knew now that they were gonna ambush Raheim. I knew that I needed to do something but I wasn't clear yet on what.

Felicia

The plane couldn't land fast enough. I walked as fast as I could to the exit sign and looked around out front for Raheim's aunt. It was already five o'clock and everything in me told me that my time was limited. Finally I saw a light brown lady wearing a black shirt and pair of jeans. She waved me over and we both met somewhere in the middle. For a moment we looked at each other and then she hugged me. I relaxed into her arms and fought back tears.

"You can put that bag in the trunk," she opened the trunk and let me place my carryon bag inside.

"Do you know where he is?" I tried to check my voice because I swear I wanted to jump out of my skin.

"Honey, things are a bit crazy right now. Amir is missing and Raheim is going to get him at 8 tonight. He looked all crazy when he came to my house, but he wanted me to know how he feels about you and he wants you taken care of."

Why did it sound like things were so final. Was she trying to say he thought he might die tonight?

"Ms. Sadie, I need to talk to Raheim today, it's important, did he tell you where he was going?"

"No, he just said he wanted me to pick you up from the airport and to make sure you were taken care of." Before she could finish her sentence I had my cell up to my ear dialing his number. All I knew is that his ass better pick up or I would be on a one-woman mission across Philly trying to find his ass. After the fourth ring his voicemail picked up telling me to kindly leave him a message.

"Raheim, WHERE ARE YOU?" I shouted before ending the call. I couldn't take this drama, not right now and especially not with a baby hanging over my fate.

"Don't worry he'll be ok," she said soothingly and I knew she thought she was helping me with that weak ass cliché, but it wasn't alright and it wouldn't be until I saw my man again. I stared at the fast moving cars whizzing by on the highway and I tried to recall any information that would help me find Raheim.

Platinum Dust

Raheim

I saw Felicia's number calling into my phone but I was sitting in Dre's car trying to clear my head. This shit was heavy and I wasn't really ready for what might happen. Dre sat with me in silence for a few minutes before speaking up.

"You know I love Amir like a brother and I will do whatever it takes to get him back. But I gotta tell you that Showboat is a real ignorant ass muthafucka. He's gonna come hardcore, especially since you already got the best of him. We gotta be smart about this shit so stick to the plan and things will work out for the best." I took a deep breath and tried not to focus on how dangerous this situation could be.

The plan was to have me go in alone with my cell phone strapped to my back. We would have Dre on the line waiting for my cue. When they heard the cue Dre and his boys would come in with guns blazing and I would grab Amir and roll out. It seemed clear cut but I knew how many things could go wrong. I didn't want to show fear, especially in front of my best friend, but the heart grows weak under pressure.

"Rah, stay cool man. You know I got your back and stop stressing. We bout to show that sucka who run this city." He held out his hand for one of our handshakes. I sure as hell hoped he was right because I didn't feel like dying today. We both stepped out of the car at the same time walking into his house in West Philly. The house was filled with a nervous energy and more than twenty dudes willing to die to save my brother. I felt humbled and appreciative because I couldn't say I would be willing to die for another man's cause.

Candy was walking around half naked passing out drinks while all eyes were locked on the table covered with every type of semi-automatic weapon imaginable. Terrance, one of Dre's boys from middle school was explaining what each weapon was capable of. He looked every man directly in the eye as he talked, leaving the crowd silent with awe. Terrance was always into guns, even when we were kids he used to sneak into his step dad's gun cabinet and just stare in amazement.

I knew I should call Felicia back but I didn't want her to talk me out of it. If I heard her voice I would crack and probably want to see her and I knew that wouldn't be good for Amir. I had to stay focused and if I made it out alive I swear I wouldn't mess with any other woman but her. A quick look down at my Cartier watch showed 6:30, it felt like the time was moving way too slow.

"Let's go," Dre stood in the middle of the dining room and shouted out his last order. Adrenaline filled my veins. I knew if I had to die to save my brother than I needed to make peace with both myself and God. I sent up a prayer asking for forgiveness. If nothing else Amir tried to show me that God would forgive even the worst of us. Everybody started heading outside to get into the five cars and trucks parked out front. Dre held my arm back so we both could stand and watch everyone load into the vehicles.

"I told you I got you right?" He looked me in the eyes.

"I love you, man," I said.

"Yeah and I love you too, man. Now enough of this girly shit, let's go take out Showboat." We jumped in his Grand Marquis and he blasted Beanie Sigel's "Feel It In The Air" track as we started the procession of cars that would bring on the destruction. The streets of Philadelphia were always busy and tonight was no different. Tall buildings provided cover for mischievous behavior and shadows were mistaken for figures. I didn't know if my mind was playing tricks on me or if I actually saw a tall dark figure staring directly through me. I closed my eyes and let the music consume me.

"You may be dead by morning," I told myself and in that brief moment I thought about me and Felicia in Jamaica. I thought about how happy she was when I said she was my woman. I thought about my visit with Janet and how I needed to save Amir so I could tell him that I went up to see her.

The old warehouse set a few feet back off the curb. There were a few cars parked out front of the building but not enough for it to be suspicious. Light came through the windows letting us know they were already there. The street was pretty much abandoned with no stray cars driving by. In unison all cars slowed down and music went off. We were there 45 minutes before 8, which gave me an advantage. Dre pulled over a few blocks down from the warehouse and got out of the car.

The drivers of each car jumped out and Dre let everybody know that they would stay parked until they heard the cue. He also said that if he heard anything foul he would leave early which made me feel better. I decided to get the party started earlier because it gave me an advantage. It would interfere with the amount of time they had to plan a counterattack. I jumped out of the car, shook Dre's hand again and stated.

"For the first time in your life, please don't be on nigga time." He nodded and he checked my cell strapped to my back and dialed his number. I started making my way down the long road leading up to the warehouse after he answered and verified that he could hear me talking. My eyes were alert for any suspicious movements on the road, but there was nothing. I felt naked without my piece but Dre insisted that it could be deadly if they did a weapons check. My heart started pounding the closer I got to the warehouse.

"Amir is in there, go get your brother," I had to coach myself to approach the door. I could hear talking on the other side and knew right away I wouldn't be the only man at the party. This made me uneasy because I only thought it would be Jackie doing the transaction. I guess Showboat was there to get a bit of pay back. I wish I could get him alone again. I would beat his ass one more time. I knocked on the door and the voices stopped and the sound of movement took its place.

"Who is it?" The familiar female voice asked.

"Raheim." what I really wanted to say was, "who the fuck do you think it is," but I held my tongue. The door was opened after a long pause leaving me feeling vulnerable. I knew I was walking into a trap but what type of trap was the question. Jackie was standing in the middle of the floor and I didn't step inside for a moment.

"I said 8'oclock now didn't I?" Jackie was much smaller than I expected, not a chick I would mess wit, but definitely not bad for a sadistic broad.

"Well when family is involved we tend to not be late." I stepped inside and braced myself for an ambush but nothing happened.

"Where's my brother?" I looked around the partially empty room and noticed three husky dudes each holding hand guns.

"You don't call any shots nigga I wanna know why the hell you think you can go breaking people's jaws." She started to walk toward me and I knew this was a setup at the same moment I could see one of the guys approaching slowly.

"Check this sucka," she ordered him.

I needed to be cool but I could feel the sweat beads popping up on my eyebrow. I knew my life was on the line if they felt the cell phone strapped to my back. One of her goons rocking a black hoodie gave me a standard pat down. His hands quickly went up and down my legs and over my arms and sides. Grateful he wasn't smart enough to check my back I had to calm my breathing.

"Where's my brother? I said I would switch places." From the glint in her eye I could tell she liked what she saw. She was searching my face and I almost wanted to smile and shake my head. She was acting gangsta for an ugly ass dude that wasn't man enough to handle his own shit.

"Yo just let me blast this nigga!" The smaller of the three guys raised his gun like he just might shoot. I never took my eyes off of Jackie.

"Boom, calm your ass down. I said I got this. Go get baby boy." With a nod of the head Boom reluctantly walked into the backroom. Within moments he came back dragging Amir by the arm. He was noticeably thinner with silver electrical tape across his mouth and his hands tied behind his back. The only clothes he had on were his boxers and a dirty wife beater. Large bruises covered his arms and shoulders.

He had a look of fear spread across his face. I read the message in his wide-eyed stare loud and clear. They were gonna play me and I had to think fast.

"You see your brother? He still living; if you want to keep it that way I'm gonna need you to strip down now."

"No hold up," I stalled for time. I could feel the hairs on the back of my neck standing on edge. I needed to move from in front of the door without appearing suspicious. "I'm not stripping down until you let my fucking brother go." I could feel the nervous energy in the room. My mind started to race but I needed to get closer to Amir. A door to the back room opened forcing me to look quickly in that direction. It was Showboat himself. He was still the same ugly muthafucka I whipped that day at the club. He strolled toward Jackie like he thought I was supposed to be scared. I knew it was about to get real serious, he had a point to prove.

"Listen, my girl said strip nigga, so it looks like you don't have a choice." He put a toothpick between his lips. I swear by the end of the night he would be choking on it.

"Listen homie, all of this dramatic shit is unnecessary. I said a trade and that is what the fuck it's gonna be." Boom was starting to pace and I knew I'd have to watch out for that trigger happy nigga..

"Fine, take him his brother." Jackie nodded to Boom to walk Amir over. It was too easy, either they were the biggest dummies on the planet or they were planning on killing us both.

"Amir you ok? I elevated my voice loud enough for him to hear me but also to signal Dre and the gang. Amir walked slower than Boom cared for so he slammed the butt of his gun into his shoulder. Amir flinched and stumbled for a moment and I flipped.

"Yo, what the fuck is wrong wit your punk ass? I swear if you didn't have that gun I'd fuck you up right now."

"But I got the gun nigga, so do something and you and your nut ass brother will be swimming in the Delaware River." I looked at Amir one last time and I shouted.

"Amir? I said are you ok?" Amir looked up from the floor and stared me straight in the eyes. He nodded again and I gave a knowing head nod but Boom picked up on our little signal and half spun.

"Yo sumthing ain't right," I swear it was something out of the matrix. His voice seemed to slow down and in that same moment Amir reached for the small gun Boom had hidden on his waist and managed to get off one round before the front door burst open. I dove forward on top of Amir before the sound of bullets could be heard over my head. Jackie's screams were bouncing off the walls.

"You ok?" I yelled near Amir's ear. One of his hands were free. He ripped off the tape leaving a bright red mark around his mouth.

"Yes," he managed to say before I grabbed the gun out of his hand and told him to crawl over to the door with me covering him in the back. For a moment I felt like I might actually make it out alive. My eyes darted back and forth across the room. Bodies were lying on the floor in a growing pool of blood and brain matter. A mess of curls on the floor let me know Jackie was put down. I searched for Dre in the crowd and saw that he was still standing. I turned to run out of the door behind Amir to the car Dre and I had parked a block away earlier for me to get away in. In the same moment I turned I saw Amir's body jerk forward and he fell to the ground. The same moment Amir fell I heard a loud scream "NO!" coming from a girl in the back of the room.

"Shit!" I dropped to my knees barely missing a bullet.

"Get up, Amir?"

"I can't," his eyes were wide with fear. This couldn't be happening. I didn't come all of this way just to lose my brother.

"Amir? Come on stay wit me." I lifted him up over my shoulder and ran us both to the exit. A piercing sting hit my arm but I didn't have time to think about it. I could hear Amir gasping for air.

"I'm gonna get you to a hospital. Hold on!" Running that block to the navy blue Honda civic was the longest distance I ever had to run.

Both car doors were unlocked as expected and I opened the back to lie Amir across the backseat.

"It burns!" Amir started to scream.

"I'm going to the hospital right now. Your cool," I reassured him. The car started up immediately and I put my foot on the gas. I felt bad for leaving Dre and his team, but my brother was shot and I couldn't risk it. I darted in an out of traffic taking the road with less streetlights. I tried to ignore the sound of Amir chocking on blood on the back seat.

"Get outta the way," I yelled at a slow driver oblivious to my situation.

"Shit! Amir don't go to sleep, you hear me? YOU AWAKE?" I yelled out to him.

"Yes..."

"Come on dude, don't go to sleep. Look I needed to tell you I saw Janet!" I glanced in the rearview mirror and saw him trying to attempt a smile. The only thing I could think to do was drive to the hospital and talk to him the whole way.

"God please let him be ok." I pleaded aloud.

If I never get an answer from God ever again in life I needed him to answer me tonight.

"Are you lying about Janet?" He asked barely above a whisper.

"No I went the day after you. She cried when she saw me. HEY! You awake?"

His eyes were closing and it started to freak me out.

"I'm tired Raheim." His voice was strained.

"NO AMIR, fight it man, where almost there, stay awake!" My foot went heavy on the gas and I raced through yellow lights and stop signs. I didn't feel relief until I saw the Mercy Fitzgerald hospital sign. I screeched to a halt in front of the emergency room entrance. The Honda looked like a toy car next to the large ambulance trucks. I jumped out of the driver's side and ran to the back of the car. "Amir, come on we here." I pulled him from the backseat his eyes were opening and closing.

"I NEED SOME HELP!!!" I ran through the automatic doors into the entrance. I didn't care about the crowd of people waiting to be seen. "My brother was shot and I need help!" I yelled to a nurse standing behind a desk.

One of the nurses sitting behind a desk paged the triage unit and ran over to help me with Amir. Within seconds a crowd of men and women wearing scrubs rushed into the ER. Two of them wheeled a gurney and I was able to lie him there. He was wheeled through the doors and disappeared down the hall. My legs wouldn't move and I needed to take a moment to catch my breath. My body felt weak and an older woman pointed to my arm.

"Son, your arm is bleeding too." After her words hit my ear my arm started to burn. I looked down at my clothes covered with blood.

"Raheim?" I looked up into the face of Felicia's friend Beverly.

"Oh my God, are you ok? Is Felicia and the baby ok?" she started looking around like she expected to find Felicia banged up beside me.

Baby? Did she say baby? My legs gave out and before I knew it I was hitting the floor.

Felicia

It has been over four hours and Raheim hasn't called me back. His aunt kept me calm by dialing all of the numbers of Raheim's friends that she knew. Most of them didn't answer or hadn't heard from him. I wanted to go out looking for him but she said it might be better if we waited for him to call. It was already past 9 o'clock and I tried not to think about him lying dead somewhere and I didn't know about it. My cell phone started ringing and I couldn't answer it fast enough.

"Felicia? Girl! What happened to Raheim?" It was Beverly and she was screaming into the phone.

"What? I haven't heard from him since earlier." I tried to conceal my irritation.

"Are you still in Jamaica?" She asked

"No, why what's wrong Bev?"

"Raheim just came into the hospital girl. He covered in blood, you betta get down here."

"What hospital?" I was frantic.

"Mercy Fitz in Darby, lil Mike broke his arm so I had to-" I hung up before she could finish her sentence.

"Raheim is at Mercy Fitzgerald, we gotta go now." I grabbed my purse and we both ran out into the car. Let him be ok God please let him be ok.

"Who was that?" his aunt asked.

"My girlfriend Beverly. She said he was covered in blood," I choked out the words. My heart was racing and my stomach tightened. I didn't tell his aunt I was pregnant and now I may not be able to tell him. This would be the worst statistic of a fatherless child because his dad was killed by violence.

"Calm down Felicia, we don't know anything yet."

"No disrespect, but you don't understand."

We finally made it to the hospital what felt like an eternity later. I was out of the car before his aunt could park. I never could figure out why so many people crowded the ER everyday. I made my way to the check in window.

"Excuse me, but I'm looking for Raheim Starz. A light skinned male that just came in."

"Ahhhh oh yeah. He is in room 10."

"Was anyone with him?" His aunt asked over my shoulder. The blond haired nurse looked down at her clipboard and nodded her head before answering.

"Yes, but he's in surgery. Are you family?"

"Yes, can I please go back now?"

She reached under the desk and buzzed us in. His aunt stayed behind asking for the name of the other person Raheim came in with. I didn't wait but walked as fast as my legs could carry me in through the double doors. The beeping sounds of breathing machines and machines that check vital signs resonated through the corridor and down into my soul. I stopped in front of the door with the number 10 beside it. I wasn't ready for what was on the other side of the door. I didn't know if he would be hooked up to machines or what I would find, but I took a deep breath and pushed through.

Raheim was lying on a bed with his eyes closed. His bloody clothes in a heap on the floor beside a guest chair. I walked up to the bed with tears in my eyes happy to see him alive. He opened his eyes and turned to face me. His face softened and he even smiled a little. Before I could lean in for a hug he reached out his hands and placed them on my stomach. I was more than surprised, but didn't have time to speak when a knock on the door interrupted the moment. A nurse escorted two young white policemen into the room.

"Do you mind if we ask you some questions?"

To Be Continued......

Sneak Peek
Part 2
Felicia's Baby

Chapter One
Raheim

I stood at the window watching my aunt Sadie and my girl Felicia step into the black limo parked in front of the house. Today was my baby brother's funeral and I didn't feel like going. With one last look in the mirror I walked through my aunt's house like a zombie. I ignored all of the well-wishers and offers of condolences from my aunt's neighbors as I stepped into the back of the limo. All eyes were on me as I sat beside Felicia. She looked good in her black knee length dress and swollen belly. It's crazy how life plays out. In the same moment I lost my brother I found out I would be a dad with the only woman I cared about in this world.

My aunt Sadie reached over and squeezed my hand. I couldn't feel anything, a week before I had to rescue my brother from a crazy bitch looking to pay me back for kicking her dude's ass. Now I was driving in the front of a funeral procession. I fought back the memory of my brother choking on his own blood in the back of a getaway car as we headed toward the church holding his body. As the limo made its way to the church I noticed how crowded the streets were. There were lots of faces I didn't recognize. Amir was well known at his church and many of its members came out to wish him farewell. I made sure his funeral was one of a kind. He had a white casket with gold plated letters spelling out his name on the side. We would even release doves when the pall bearers carried his casket to the hearse. When the limo parked in front of the church we stepped out and I forced my legs to push me forward. Family would get a private viewing and then they would allow others to come in.

My girl Felicia stood beside me the entire time holding my hand. When I stopped walking she stopped also. She knew how hard this was for me. Amir was my only brother from a mother I hated for killing my father and kicking me out of the house at eleven and a father who was dead way before his time. My aunt walked into the front of the church toward the casket and I could hear her crying loudly. I choked back the lump growing in my throat as I waited for her to come back out. Moments later she walked out with mascara lines running down her face. I knew this was hard for my aunt, first losing my dad her- only brother, then her husband a few years ago, and now, my brother that she raised like a son.

When I was finally able to muster up enough courage to go in the large room I inched forward with slow deliberate steps. Felicia hung back to close the doors to give me privacy.

I walked up to the casket closing my eyes for a moment. I couldn't believe how peaceful he looked. His hair was freshly cut and his all white suit looked good on him. I had to admit he was a pretty good looking kid. His last words 'Are you lying about seeing Janet?' rushed into my mind like a rushing river knocking me to my knees. He was happy knowing that I went to visit our mom Janet after all of the years of trying to reunite us.

I cried uncontrollably at the feet of my brother's casket. Felicia stood beside me stroking my hair.

God I asked you to let him be ok! I couldn't believe this shit. How could he be dead? I could only be mad at myself. The doors opened but I didn't look up until I felt Felicia's grip on my shoulder tighten.

Janet Starz escorted by two correctional officers walked in wearing a black two piece dress suit in true dramatic form. She walked to the casket like she couldn't believe what she was seeing. She lye across Amir's body weeping like she was the only one there. For a moment I felt sorry for the lady I grew to hate over the last 15 years. After her crying spell she stood up and wiped Amir's suit.

"Raheim, how you holding up?" she asked and I wanted to ignore her question but I could feel Felicia watching me. I stood up off the floor and did what my brother would have wanted and wrapped my arms around the same woman who threw me out into the streets. I only let her cry into my shoulder for a few moments before I pushed her back and said.

"Sorry for the loss of your only son." I could feel the venom pulsing through her blood as she stared at me with hatred. Janet Starz was only an egg donor and my brother's death wouldn't change that. I reached for my girl's hand and turned to leave the viewing room.

"Let's go find my mom."

About the Author

K.C Blaze is a passionate writer of urban tales. She spends most of her time creating new action packed stories for her readers to enjoy. With a degree in Psychology she has blended her love of the human mind with her love of writing to come up with what she hopes is a different type of urban fiction. An urban Fiction that goes a step beyond the glamorized living to touch issues in the African-American community.

31326073R00086

Made in the USA
Lexington, KY
07 April 2014